WET DREAMS ON LOCKDOWN

The Female C.O

TELIA TEANNA

URBAN AINT DEAD

Email: urbanaintdead@gmail.com

ISBN: 979-8-9902387-3-2

CONTENTS

SOUNDTRACKS

Scan the QR Code below to listen to the Soundtracks/Singles of some of your favorite U.A.D titles:

Don't have Spotify or Apple Music?
No Sweat!
Visit your choice streaming platform and search URBAN AINT DEAD.

Currently on lock serving a bid?
JPay, iHeartRadio, WHATEVER!
We got you covered.

Simply log into your facility's kiosk or tablet, go to music and search URBAN AINT DEAD.

URBAN AINT DEAD

Like & Follow us on social media:
FB - URBAN AINT DEAD
IG: @urbanaintdead
Tik Tok - @urbanaintdead

SUBMISSIONS

Submit the first three chapters of your completed manuscript to urbanaintdead@gmail.com, subject line: Your book's title. The manuscript must be in a .doc file and sent as an attachment. The document should be in Times New Roman, double-spaced, and in size 12 font. Also, provide your synopsis and full contact information. If sending multiple submissions, they must each be in a separate email. Have a story but no way to submit it electronically? You can still submit to URBAN AINT DEAD. Send in the first three chapters, written or typed, of your completed manuscript to:

URBAN AINT DEAD

P.O Box 448

Maybrook, NY 12543

DO NOT send original manuscript. Must be a duplicate.
Provide your synopsis and a cover letter containing your full contact information.
Thanks for considering URBAN AINT DEAD.

"*You have reached the voicemail of–*" Zyan sighed heavily and hung up the phone as he shook his head. He had attempted to call his girlfriend McKenzie for the third time in the last hour and he had yet to get an answer. The last that he had heard from her, she had mentioned that Zyair, his twin brother, was going to be stopping by to see her.

He hated to think about his twin brother being with his girl, but seeing as Zyan was serving a three-year bid on a manslaughter charge, it had its benefits, mostly monetary, but over the last couple of weeks, he had begun to notice some changes in McKenzie's attitude and behavior. While he wasn't surprised by her switch up in attitude, it did still hurt him. Zyan had long since prepared for McKenzie to start acting differently, that's just how it went when you were locked up behind the wall, but there were some factors that made her switch up sting more than he had expected.

The phone screen lighting up caught his attention and broke him from his thoughts. She was finally calling him back. He answered the phone but didn't say anything, his mood already sour.

"I'm sorry, you already know how yo brother is, I tried to answer an–"

Before she could finish speaking, Zyan cut her off. "What he give you?"

"Three bands..."

"Send me a screenshot."

"Okay..."

He didn't say anything else, just hung up the phone. He didn't want to hear any excuses. He was already frustrated out of his mind. He was only a couple of months into his bid, and he was still coming to terms with the way that he had ended up there in the first place. McKenzie had played a big part in it and there she was slacking in her obligations to him for his brother. Of course, it made him feel some kind of way.

It wasn't a complete or fair judgment of McKenzie's situation, though. Most of the ill feelings that Zyan felt regarding the arrangement that he had set up between Zyair and McKenzie had nothing to do with McKenzie herself, but rather the strained relationship that he had with his twin brother. There were a lot of unspoken and unresolved feelings and trauma when it came to the brothers and neither of them had a healthy way of expressing those feelings. So instead of addressing the issues, they ignored them and moved forward as if nothing bothered them at all. That's what their family had always done. It seemed to work enough.

Moments later, a screenshot showing that Zyair had sent McKenzie three-thousand-dollars for an hour of her time came through. Zyan reacted to the screenshot and then exited out of his text messages. He felt a little better after seeing their new balance. He couldn't really be mad because she handled the business, but it still annoyed him that she didn't answer his calls. He just didn't like that shit.

Zyan had decided that while he was locked up, he was going to make the most of his time and sell some work. As a team effort, McKenzie would do her part and do what she did best; get niggas to trick on her and then Zyan would flip it. It was not much different than what they had been doing before. There was just distance and a cage between them now. And with all the time that they had been spending together lately, he would say his brother was also a new contributor to the distance between them. Subconsciously, it hurt him in a way that hadn't registered to him yet, because it was difficult for him to even fathom that McKenzie would hurt him like that. He felt himself getting emotional every time he thought about it, so he would immediately busy himself with another thought instead.

He rolled his shoulders; they were feeling tense with all of his stress. He was still adjusting to his new home for the next two years and he the constant tightness in his body thanks to always being on high alert. He needed to relieve some of his stress. Deciding to calm his nerves a bit, he got off his cot to put some tissue in his door, signaling that he needed privacy and to let his celly, Pressure, know that he was busy. After that, he made himself comfortable back on his cot, put his headphones on, and then proceeded to pull his dick out and went to his favorite porn site.

Scrolling through his favorite ebony category, he spent a few minutes contemplating what he wanted to watch. Once he found something suitable, Zyan greased up his dick and pleasured himself to a video of an amateur couple roleplaying as a female officer and an inmate. The video had caught his eye, it was a relatable fantasy and had piqued his interest when he saw it.

In typical porn fashion, the acting wasn't all that great, but the concept was still arousing. He was patient, slowly stroking his hardened length as he watched the scene be set up. It was only a matter of minute until the corny lines were minimal and the fucking was at its maximum. It wouldn't be on and crackin' by then.

A light sheen of sweat coated Zyan's face as his pleasure and arousal grew as he watched the thick almond skinned female officer with a crotchless cop uniform on with a utility belt and a pair of handcuffs dangled from her small waist, repeatedly take back-shots from the inmate dressed in an orange jumpsuit. He could feel himself getting close to his climax.

He was so caught up in his fantasy and the video that he hadn't heard the knock on the door until it was opening.

"Aye man! What the fu– oh... What you want?" Zyan sat up and quickly tucked his dick back into his shorts and jumped down from his bunk. He was thrown off his square when he saw a pretty female C.O. closing the door behind her caught his attention.

She was a short thing, stood about five-foot-five, roughly weighed somewhere between two-hundred-seventy-five-pounds, and had rich cocoa colored skin. Even in her uniform he could tell that she was curvaceous. Her voice when she spoke had his dick straining in his shorts.

"My bad. I knocked a couple times, and I got no answer. Pressure told me to leave these with you." She pulled her tucked shirt out of her pants and pulled a couple of black wrapped cans from out of her clothes.

Zyan lifted his eyebrows in response and nodded his confirmation. He had never seen the officer before and he was curious as to when she had gotten there, and how Pressure already had her dropping packs off to him. "Aight, coo." He said and grabbed each of the cans she passed to him.

"Sorry to, uh, interrupt." The officer giggled, at the tent in his shorts. She swung the ponytail that she had her small box braids pulled into over her shoulder and then slipped out of Zyan's cell and away from his door. Standing at the door, he watched her through the small window of his cell as she made her way out of the dorm, watching the feminine way that she swung her hips with each step and stroked himself while he watched her. He wished he would have asked her to watch him, but she had caught him so off guard he didn't have much time to think of much else other than to play off the fact that she had caught him beating his meat.

She didn't seem to mind it, though.

Once she was no longer in his line of view, Zyan made himself comfortable on his cot again and finished watching his porn video, a pretty new face etched in his mind as he watched the sexy officer get fucked by the inmate until he nutted hard all over his lower abs and his thumb. After his release, he felt much better and could think a little more clearly. It was exactly what he needed to help him regain his focus.

After cleaning himself and his mess up, he took the tissue out of your door and then continued on with the rest of the things he had planned to get done that night. He made a mental note to ask Pressure about the female officer once he came back to their cell. He was very interested in finding out how he had managed to pull that off.

SULANI SIGHED as she pulled her braids out of the tight ponytail, she had them pulled into. She had just gotten off work and was walking to her car when she groaned at the tall and stocky build leaning against the side of her Audi. "Will you just leave me the hell alone? Clearly, I don't wanna be bothered, Dolo."

"That's what we do now? You really that mad at me that you went and changed your *whole* shift just to get away from me, Su? I thought we was better than that, baby. Why you tryna hurt me?" Sulani's longtime on-and-off-again boyfriend, Darius "Dolo" Samuels.

Sulani rolled her eyes as she walked up to the driver's side door which Dolo stood in front of, blocking her from getting inside. Dusk was about to break as the sun began to rise above the horizon. For just under two years, Sulani had been working at the prison but mostly worked during the day shift. She was a female Corrections Officer, but she had a way with the people from Wardens to Lieutenants and even Judges. She was well connected and that allowed her to move throughout the prison as she wanted to and gave her a special ability to fly under the radar while she was there.

That was until she started dating Dolo and his arrogant attitude and constant need to brag started bringing unwanted and certainly unnecessary attention her way. There was a code of silence that any man that she dealt with had to abide by. The industry that they were in was all about reputation and networking. Her network was extensive, but many of those relationships came with their own codes of conduct, rules, and expectations.

Sulani knew the game, and she knew how to play it well.

The same couldn't be said for Dolo, though. He had been doing the most as of late, threatening to beat up niggas that were attempting to talk to her, to starting petty arguments with inmates and coworkers while they were on the clock. There was just too much bullshit that he was causing and attaching to her name. She had to separate herself from him immediately. Talking to him had been something he had made impossible, so her leaving him was her only other option.

"Okay, and? You hurt me, too. So where does that leave us?" She put her hand on her hip. Her lanyard with her car and house keys attaching to it jingling as they dangled from her hip.

"Why can't we talk about it?"

"I tried to talk to you about it and you kept saying that it was just in my head. You acting like you don't hear the whispers, but I do. And I know damn sure it just ain't just in my head. You talk too much, and you don't know how to listen, either so I'm good. I want no more parts of you or anything that you have going on. I have a bad taste in my mouth about it all, so I'm good you and on us. We ain't have no business fuckin' around anyway." She admitted. She sounded exhausted, as if she was long since tired of talking about it. And she was.

Sulani was beyond over all of the drama that had been going on in her life. The only thing that was left for her to do was to set boundaries and to stand on them. That was the key to her gaining the peace that her soul was craving for. One way or another she would learn the lesson.

"You don't mean that." The male officer attempted to grab Sulani by the hand, but she tucked it away by crossing her arms over her chest.

"I said exactly what I meant." Her tone was void of any emotion. She had already accepted the situation for what it was and there wasn't much more that she had to say. He just wanted to keep it going since he was refusing to see their reality for what it was.

Toxic.

Dolo pointed a finger in her direction. "I know what this is about..." Sulani could see his facial features harden. Their eyes were locked in a cold gaze, and it was then that the resentment that he held towards her clear as day. She couldn't see it before then, but she was sure that she wouldn't be able to miss it again.

A slight chill shook her spine at the realization.

"You mad about that shit that happened with your family..." He said accusatorially.

Sulani sucked her teeth, rolled her eyes, and shifted her weight onto one foot. "Here you go..." She let out a long sigh. The thudding of her heart was loud in her ears as she felt her blood begin to boil. He was purposely trying to get under her skin. She knew what he was doing so he wasn't going to feed into his bullshit. "Can you move so I can go home, now?" She waved her hand through the air as if she was shoo-ing him away.

Dolo pushed himself off her car and opened the door for her. He pressed his thick, purple lips together. Dolo's skin was so dark he almost looked purple. While he wasn't an "ugly" man, he was definitely interesting looking. As a child he often got comparisons to a gorilla and strangely was part of what appealed to Sulani about him the most.

Her curiosity to find out if he was just as much a gorilla in the bedroom as he looked and at even times behaved to be. Thinking with her pussy had gotten her into some bullshit and she was beginning to regret her choice when she had failed to keep things under her control.

Sulani had given Dolo one too many sniffs of her pussy and the nigga turned into King Kong. He was going crazy about his bitch and that wasn't something she had signed up for.

Possessive hadn't been a trait that she could see in him beforehand. Had she known it before being intimate with him, she would have avoided him all together.

She had been learning that Dolo was a lot smarter than he let on, and even had his own way of being able to find out information and accomplish his aims. The more she saw of him, the more she saw that he was borderline psychotic. He was turning out to be much more of a problem than she had expected. Wordlessly, Sulani got in her car and Dolo rolled her window down before he shut the door.

"It's okay." Dolo said then leaned through the window and kissed her on the side of her temple. "We gon' figure it out. Get home safe, I'll see you later."

Sulani sighed deeply, frustrated that he really wasn't getting that she didn't want to be with him anymore, but instead of saying anything about it, she gave him a sarcastic thumbs up, and then started her car. The last thing she felt like doing was arguing with him about them not being in a relationship with each other anymore. What she really wanted to do was go home, eat, and then take her ass to sleep. She'd deal with him and all of his bullshit later.

After pulling out of her parking space, she watched Dolo disappear back into the prison facility through her rearview mirror, then made her way home. Thirty minutes later she was pulling into her assigned parking spot of the apartment that she stayed in and made her way inside. As soon as she shut the door behind her, she reached her arms behind her back and slipped her hands under her shirt and unhooked her bra. "Mmm." She moaned when she pulled her straps off her shoulders and the cups from her titties. The relief she got from freeing her breasts from their temporary holding cell was at the top of her favorite sensations list.

Then she proceeded to make her way to the bathroom where she started the shower and began to strip out of her work clothes. She preferred to come home and shower right away. It was always necessary for her to wash the stench of prison off her before she did anything else. After a good ol' hour shower, Sulani got out of the shower, dried majority of her body, wrapped her naked frame in the towel, then made her way into her kitchen.

Looking in the refrigerator, Sulani hummed to herself, Goapele's "Closer," had been in her head on repeat since she had gotten in the shower. She hadn't put on any music before she got in, but the song had popped into her head, and she had been humming and vibing to the tune since it popped into her mind.

She grabbed her phone and went to the Spotify app and put the song on while she made herself breakfast. It was nearing eight AM and she wanted to get something in her body before she laid down and got some rest. She had another shift later that night.

After she made herself a breakfast sandwich of her favorite buttermilk white bread, a fried egg, hash browns, sausage, some turkey bacon and topped it off with some ketchup. She poured herself a tall glass of some Cran-Apple juice and sat on her living room couch.

Sulani two-bedroom apartment was nicely decorated. The color scheme of her home was a mix of creams, reds, and pinks. Her couches were blood red and decorated with cream throw pillows and blankets. The color combination was striking to most, but everything about her home décor from the varieties of paintings and pictures of various fruits and other objects to the fancy cherrywood furniture pieces. It was strange but fitting for the mysterious woman.

She turned on her TV, loaded up Netflix and turned on the TV show *You* while she ate her food. While she was watching the show, her mind drifted off when a sex scene came on influencing her to have dirty thoughts. Immediately the memory of when she walked into Pressure and his celly's room and saw his celly stuffing his hard dick back into his pants. The large tent was imprinted into her mind, and she couldn't help the way she salivated at the mental image.

The thudding of her clit between her bare thighs was hard for her to ignore. She was sitting with her legs cocked open. She licked her lips when a slight breezed licked her sensitive and exposed private area. Her nipples tightened and the slight friction of the hardened buds rubbing against the abrasive material of her towel only further aroused her. After finishing her sandwich, Sulani rushed to the kitchen, rinsed her plate, threw it into the dishwasher, washed her hands, then hurried to her bedroom. She made sure to snatch her phone off of the sink in the bathroom as she passed it.

Sulani dropped her towel to the floor and jumped into her bed and threw her fluffy white comforter and sheets back. Her room was dark thanks to the fact that she had blackout curtains drawn, just as she preferred it. Settling herself on her back, she bit her lip as she opened up the *Gmail* app and scrolled until she saw the email that she had received early that morning.

It was a newsletter blast from *BLKTouch,* a pro-black adult film production company. With her subscription, Sulani had access to new black porn videos each month. For twelve dollars a month she loved that she had access to new, sexy scenarios that never failed to help her catch a big "O." Once she was in a comfortable position, she pressed play on the new scene, and put a hand between her cocked thighs. She slowly began rubbing her clit as the scenario played out. A young woman was new in her apartment complex and the neighbor's sexy man turned out to be a temptation that she couldn't resist.

For thirty minutes Sulani rubbed her clit to the video occasional thoughts of Zyan and his third leg plaguing her mind as she got herself right with the aid of the tastefully made porno until she was climaxing and gasping for breath and dripping with sweat. By the time she had finished, Sulani's fingers were drenched in her sticky arousal.

Once she had caught her breath, she lazily rolled out of her bed and went to the bathroom where she peed, cleaned herself up, and then made her way back into bed, her body officially exhausted and spent. Her lights were out as soon as her head hit the pillow.

Chapter 2

"And you said his homie's name is Zyan?" Sulani asked as she slipped on her work uniform, slipping the tan shirt on after she had her bra in place.

"Oh yeah, Zyan is hella coo. Him and Pressure been friends for a good lil minute now. They been trappin' since forever. They was who McKenzie and I would get all those pills from back when we used to sell them in college." The silky voice on the other end of the phone said. "McKenzie is his girl, you know? You remember my best friend, right?"

"Gemini, you know good and damn well I don't remember none of yo fifty million little friends." Sulani chuckled at her younger cousin. A true loner at heart, it was true that Sulani couldn't recall any of the friends that her cousin had brought around her. Gemini's friend group was the complete opposite of the crowd that she usually rolled with. "I do remember McKenzie, though. You talkin' about yo *ex-girlfriend* McKenzie?"

The giggle Gemini let out confirmed that she was correct, though the words that left her mouth told a different story. "If you're talking about the McKenzie I have been rumored to have dated, then yeah, that McKenzie."

Sulani smirked and sucked her teeth. "Bitch, please. Y'all gay ass bitches..."

"I *know* you ain't talkin' *Mrs. Officer.*" Gemini's tinkling laugh made Sulani laugh with her.

"Aye, aye, aye... we ain't talkin' about that right now." If she could have blushed, she would have been. Sulani had done her experimenting throughout college and had done even more once she had graduated and began working at a women's prison. She had done her fair share of dibbling and dabbling into forbidden territory. She enjoyed flirting with disaster too much.

Far too much.

"Anyway, McKenzie's his girl, huh? Interesting... they exclusive?"

"I mean..." she drew out the last word. "It's McKenzie... It's *us,* ya know?" She was speaking in code.

Sulani was stepping into her pants when she hummed her understanding. "Mmm... right. So, I guess it's safe to say he got a lil motion... Yo girl would be trippin' if he stepped out?"

"Girl, McKenzie know her nigga, and her nigga know his

hoe. That's just how it is around here. I'm sure it ain't much different than how me and P operate. Kenzie is kinda trippin' right now, though. Between you and me, shit been gettin' serious between his brother and McKenzie, though. I'm kind of worried for her. That shit *can't* end well." Gemini was vomiting at the mouth at that point.

"He got a brother, and his girl is fuckin' him?" Sulani's eyebrows raised in surprise.

"A twin brother! And yeah, he's just another trick, though. Zyan wouldn't go for that shit. It's only even happening because the nigga gon' pay that fee." Gemini gossiped.

"So... homeboy is a P?" Sulani had to clarify.

"Oh, hell nah! Zyan ain't like that... but... he is the one in charge of their finances."

Sulani shook her head. "Tuh... couldn't be me..." She couldn't imagine giving a man that kind of control over her. She had done it once, and she had long since vowed that another man could never get that kind of access to her again. That was a lesson she'd only have to learn once.

"That's what they all say. Don't play my bitch, though. She been through a lot. No matter what, she's gonna do what she needs to do to survive. Like the rest of us, we're all just doing what we know best based on the knowledge that we have. Hoeing is all she knows." Gemini defended her friend, and Sulani respected it and her position.

"I hear you, cuz. I feel you, too. You already know me. Been there, done that. Ain't no judgement here." Sulani clarified her response. It hadn't been a jab at her friend, but rather a negative response to her own personal trigger. It should have been a thought that she kept in her head. "That's crazy she catchin' feelings for the twin. That's gotta be a fucked-up ass feeling. Him and his brother close?"

"Hm... you sure seem interested... don't tell me you liked what you saw when you went and dropped that pack off yesterday." Gemini laughed, already knowing her cousin.

"I mean, the nigga is fine! Nothin' but dark chocolate and every time I think about him, I always imaging me smearing my pussy all over his fuckin' face..." Sulani let out a soft sigh, daydreaming about smothering the man with her coochie.

Gemini's laugher filled her ears again and she smiled as she went to the kitchen after she finished getting dressed and packed herself a quick lunch, a frozen hot pocket, a snack pack bag of Cheetos, a nectarine, and a strawberry lemonade. She put them in a lunch bag that she purchased to keep her food cool in the fridge throughout the day. The bag had her name on it and if anyone were to take something out of it before she could get to it, she could know.

"You silly as hell, Su. Shit, do you, cuz. Ain't none of my business anyway."

"Is he coo for real, though? He gotta be because I ain't heard nun about him since I been here. He must be low key and flyin' under the radar." Sulani needed to know exactly what she was dealing with before she walked into some bull-shit. Niggas were good at cappin'. Gemini was the perfect person to ask about Zyan. If a nigga was relevant and had motion or not was a question that she could trust her favorite cousin to give her an accurate answer.

"Yeah, I guess you can say that. Zyan's a smoove nigga, though. He kinda hot headed. He likes to fight. Like McKenzie, he's about a bag. His street name is Ice. Normally he keeps a mouth full of diamonds, but it's said he's quick to put a muthafucka on ice, too. But you know... that's what the streets say. He solid in my opinion."

Sulani made mental notes of the information that her cousin was given her. Her curiosity had been piqued, but so far, she liked what she saw. It also helped that he had a good rep with Pressure and her cousin. Sulani liked Pressure. He was a smart dude and solid in his own right. He always moved to the beat of his own drum, had great people skills, and was stood on principles. The way that she saw it, he was a good pick for her cousin. He just couldn't seem to stay out of jail long enough to do something productive. She still had high hopes for him though.

If Zyan was in good with Pressure, then she knew that he had to be worth something. "That's all I needed to hear." Sulani said as she put on her windbreaker and grabbed her keys off of the hook near the door and locked her front door before she began to make her way to her car.

"Good luck, cuz," Gemini laughed. "Don't get into too much trouble. You know you. One day that good luck of yours is gonna run out."

"Uh, uh! Don't be sayin' that shit out loud! Let me knock on some muthfuckin' wood!" She hustled over to a tree a few feet away from her car and rapped her knuckles against the growing tree alongside the walkway.

"Yeah, yeah. Call me if you need me." Gemini said. That's how she usually ended all of her phone calls, which was something that she appreciated. She could always expect her cousin to be there for her if she needed her.

"Yup! Later, loser." Sulani said and hung up her phone as she climbed into her car.

Her cousin had come through with some decent information to help her with her budding interest in Zyan. It was no coincidence that she had ended up a corrections officer. Her late father Lawrence Evans was a Warden who was at the height of his career at the time of his death when he was shot and killed during a gas station robbery gone wrong.

Sulani knew her father though. He was no saint and let her in on the innerworkings of the prison systems and the opportunities to make some *real* money.

Illegal money.

As a single father raising a young girl on his own, he taught her young that transparency was an undervalued trait.
her young that transparency was an undervalued trait.

"When you're always honest, transparent, and real no matter what it looks like, it will keep your hands clean. The truth shall always set you free..."

As a result, he was always open with his daughter about

exactly what he had going on when he worked at the prison. From smuggling in drugs and contraband, to covering up and executing murders, Lawrence Evans had done it all in the thirty-seven years he contributed to the prison system.

His death had long been something he had prepared for. When his time came, Sulani shed a few tears of sadness but had moved on pretty quickly. She loved and missed him, but in her eyes, Lawrence was a good man who had taught her well. It was because of him that she knew that she was built for whatever.

Sulani was able to accept the fate of her dad not being there for her anymore, but she was grateful to have the time she had with him and experience what it was like to be loved on by a well-intentioned man. He wasn't perfect, but she knew he loved her and made many sacrifices to give her a better chance at life and a fair chance at true happiness. What more could she have asked of him?

Once he was gone, Sulani had been there to pick up where her father had left off. Before his murder, he had made sure that she knew and was introduced to everyone that she needed to, to keep everything running smoothly throughout the prison. She now played a vital role in the illegal operations throughout the prison, but there were a select few who knew just how involved she was in drugs, cellphones, and other forbidden contraband being smuggled into the facility.

Since she was a teenager, Lawrence had laced his daughter with enough game to know how to move when she was on the inside. He taught her to use logic to be able to keep up with the witty and crafty inmates, while using her femininity to disarm even the most untrusting of men.

The twenty-five-year-old was one of a kind and certainly comfortable in her skin. Sulani lived an interesting life, and she genuinely loved her job. Nearly every day was an adventure for her. With the way she had been trained to move, her days were more unpredictable than most would think.

Thirty minutes later, she was making her way into the facility. She wasn't scheduled to bring anything in that day, so she went in through the usual staff entrance where she was pat down and then walked through the metal detector. The time that she was spending working in the specific compound that she was one with the least amount of issues. That turned out to be a good thing for her because it meant that she could hide there from Dolo.

Arrogant and attention seeking, she could always count on Dolo's pride to keep him busy in the more dangerous, ignorant, and deadly dorms. Never one to miss out on an opportunity to assert and flex his dominance and power, Sulani wasn't concerned with him coming to bother her anytime soon.

She had pulled some strings to be able to get put in her new seat in the body heat of another person near her back end as she bent over to slide her lunch in a spot on the bottom row of the refrigerator.

"Look who we have here... I been waiting on yo fine ass to

come down here... What do I owe the pleasure?" Dennis, another correctional officer at the facility.

When Sulani stood to her full height and turned around, she dramatically rolled her eyes at his comments. "I forgot yo weird ass was down here. Ew." She said dismissively and side-stepped the short, light-skinned chubby man with a shiny bald head and closed the opened refrigerator door. She did it as a polite way of creating distance between them without offending him and the inappropriate conversation he was attempting to have with her.

Dennis was one of Dolo's opps. Once upon a time, the two of them had been friends but that had changed once Dennis attempted to backdoor him, and snatch homeboy's girl. The moment Sulani had told Dolo that he tried to force himself on her while in the break room, the following day, Dolo beat his ass right in front of their LT. As a result of the incident, Dennis had been moved to a place where he couldn't cause too much trouble.

The incident had happened seven months prior, and it looked like it was about to be another full circle moment. While she hadn't been wrong in revealing the fact that Dennis had attempted to make his move on her, not mentioning the situation at all would have spared her another situation that she left unresolved.

"Aww, you not happy to see me, Su? I took an ass whoopin' for you and you don't even be showin' a nigga no love..." He dramatically sniffled. "That really hurts my feelings. I thought you were a good person but now I just think you're a bully. Why you make your boyfriend beat me up?"

Sulani was leaving the break room when she spoke. "Keep fuckin' with me and I'ma bully yo ass alright."

It would have been useless to continue entertaining the man and his shenanigans. Sulani was aware that Dennis was all cap and that his word weighed nothing. He was a lame nigga that liked to talk shit. And being that he stood at the same height as her, but weighed slightly more than she did, she didn't worry about him at all. He wasn't anything that she couldn't handle, weapon or not.

Soon after, Sulani got herself settled in the booth, with a good book and got comfortable. She was at a point in her career that even though she loved it, she was getting a little tired of all the toxic bullshit that came with it.

When she first started at her job two years prior, her father had instructed her to remain lowkey and to not draw too much attention to herself. Never to have known him to be a liar, she had done as he told her to, and it had been working out for her.

Her daddy had never told her in the wrong.

LATER IN HER SHIFT, she was getting ready to do count when a knock at the door of the dorm that she was monitoring caught her attention. Leaving her spot in the booth, Sulani made her way to the door and felt a flood of irritation surge through her when she saw who was standing behind the door. After taking a deep breath, she raised her eyebrows at Zyan.

He hadn't done anything to irritate her for real, he didn't know her or the way she preferred to deal with inmates. Everything she did had to be lowkey and calculated. Her logic told her that's how she was able to get ahead in life.

But in a world where everyone had their demons, Sulani's demon in particular had turned her into an attention whore. Good, bad, or indifferent, if someone was to show her some attention, she had no problem entertaining them as long as they played by her rules.

Approaching her while she was working was a big no for Sulani. It was a rule that her father had been strict on her about implementing thanks to an incident where she was reported to have been intimate with a woman over the women's pod. Her father had to pull some strings for her in order to save her from prison time and her job. It was the first time she had majorly fucked up and the disappointment she saw in her dad's face killed her and she vowed that she would never disappoint him like that again.

Her dad being mad at her was something she couldn't stand for long. She was his only child, his heart, and she knew it. He thought so highly of her, yet still, she had ways about her that caused her to self-sabotage. When he had received the news that one of the female inmates at the prison his daughter was working at had filed a complaint against her for "abusing her authority," and sexually assaulting her,

Lawrence had to call in a few favors to make the call go away.

Sulani had been able to stay out of trouble ever since, for the most part. Her first year into her job as a C.O. at a women's prison, she had gotten caught up with the wrong bitch in the women's dorm. A couple of naughty rendezvous she had with the woman had the bitch acting crazy in love.

Desiree, the inmate Sulani had been intimate with, had been locked up for four years and had taken an immediate interest the moment she laid eyes on Sulani. She made it her mission to speak to her every time she saw her. Desiree was generous in her compliments and often knew exactly what to say to make Sulani feel good and feed her ego.

Quickly, Sulani was able to see that Desiree, a beautiful fair skinned woman, with a large more of curly black hair, really had an infatuation with her. Because she lacked knowledge of herself at that time, she couldn't see that her intentions of getting involved with the inmate were not pure. Not completely, at least. She just enjoyed the attention that she got from the woman.

Sulani was new and fresh in the prison and her job as a Correctional Officer when she met Desiree. For eight months, multiple times a week she would sneak into the inmate's cell and other hidden places so that they could be intimate. Once she got bored, Sulani broke things off with Desiree and it didn't play out well.

It was when she walked into work that day and sever

police officers were there, waiting for her to arrive, that she realized she fucked up. Her stomach dropped and for the first time she became aware of the fact that she was a very reckless person who was always swayed by temporary and fleeting feelings and interests.

Not too much had changed though. Sulani just set more boundaries, became stricter on her rules and thought all of her moves all the way through.

Zyan approaching her was not something she expected, let alone thought through. With everything she had going, she didn't want to give anyone a reason to come fucking with her. She wasn't the only one with connections.

Snitches were everywhere and she was sure it was only going to be a matter of time before the news got back to Dolo and he did something stupid.

"Wassup?" She asked him, the mental image of the tent in his pants the day before stuck in her mind. She licked her lips as she took in his handsome face.

"I just came to speak since I was over here." He said, leaning his forearm against the door and then resting his forehead, a sexy smirk on his face that made Sulani's heart skip a beat and her clit thump with need.

Sulani shook her head at his antics. "Mm," one side of her mouth pulled to the side and then she pursed her lips, a clear indication of her dismay at his reply. "I appreciate that... that your way of showing your interest?"

Zyan's eyebrows shot up at her question. "Who said I was

interested?" He asked a question of his own. Though he was interested, he wasn't going to admit that when her energy towards him seemed off.

Sulani smirked at his response, softening up a bit. "You right. What can I do for you, sir?" She asked, batting her eyelashes at him dramatically.

Zyan blinked at the woman's change in her demeanor. He hadn't really thought his plan through. Stopping to talk to her hadn't been something that he had planned to do. He had left his cell briefly to make a run and saw the sexy C.O. sitting in the booth and decided to stop and talk to her. After regaining his composure, Zyan's smirk returned. "There's a lot that you could do for me, sweetie." His eyes drifted down to her chest, a mental image of what he imagines her large breasts looked like underneath all of her clothes.

Sulani wrinkled her nose at his reply and smiled cutely at him, a cute giggle bubbled up from her chest. "Sweetie? That's cute. I can guarantee that I am anything but sweet." The mischievous grin that followed her reply made Zyan's dick jump.

"Well, shiiit, I'm tryna find out." He bit his lip.

Sulani licked her lips again, her eyes darting around him to observe what was going on behind him. She didn't want to be standing at the door too long. The longer she talked to him, the higher the chances of someone becoming suspicious and informing Dolo of her chat with him got. That was the last thing she needed. She didn't need any more drama in her life.

"Look," she sighed and locked eyes with him, "I got a lot going on. You know what's up. Moving forward, don't come talk to me here. I'm kinda hot, right now. I'ma text Pressure and let him know to give you my number. Okay?"

Zyan dropped his forearm from the door and pushed away from it, slowly backing away from the door, nodding his understanding. That's all he needed to hear.

"Ugh!" Sulani groaned as she closed the book that she was reading after slipping her bookmark between the pages of it to mark where she had left off. She still had a few hours of her shift left and she could hardly focus on the words that she was reading. Her mind had been reeling, multiple different things distracting her from enjoying her book.

A heavy sigh escaped her lips as she leaned back in her chair and leaned her head back against the chair. There was a heaviness in her spirit that she couldn't quite pinpoint what had caused it. She felt emotionally depleted and each day she found it a little harder to get out of the bed. She had lost the only person that she knew loved her more than life, and though she knew that the day would come, it still didn't keep her from waking up each morning, turning over to grab her phone and scroll through the many memories that she had left of her favorite person. Her father.

The sound of her phone buzzing against the desk that she was sitting at caught her attention and she picked it up.

It was a text from a random number:

???: Lock me in, Sexy...

Sulani smirked after reading the message, perking up a bit.

Sulani: Done...

Zyan: You been having a good day?

Sulani: My day been smoove. Thanks. How's yours?

Zyan: I ain't got no complaints...

Sulani rolled her eyes at his dry reply.

Sulani: Look... I'm not a fan of the small talk. You ain't gotta beat around the bush with me, babe. So, wassup? What is it exactly that you want from me?

Not one who liked dealing with formalities, she preferred to get straight to the point. Zyan was an inmate in prison, she already had it made up in her mind that he wanted *something* from her. They all did.

Zyan: Damn, why a nigga gotta want something from you?

Sulani: So, you saying you don't?

Zyan: I ain't saying that at all. I just wanna know why that's the first thing on your mind. Maybe I just wanna get to know you...

Sulani: Am I wrong, though? I know you want something from me, y'all always do. So why waste time trying to "get to know me" when you could just tell me what you

want, and I can either choose whether or not I want to be involved. You already know what I'm about.

Ten minutes went by before she got another reply.

Zyan: You ain't wrong... it's a lot I want from you to be so real... I need a mule...

Zyan: I want some of that pussy, too.

Zyan: And to put this dick down your throat.

Zyan: Fuck all your holes...

Oh, my Lord... She thought to herself as she read each message that came through. Immediately, she began to feel her pussy pulse with need at the thought of the fine ass dark chocolate that was Zyan Jackson. The image of the large tent in his shorts brought itself back to the forefront of her thoughts.

Sulani squeezed her thighs together, applying pressure to her throbbing clit. A hyper-sexual woman, she loved to fuck and be fucked. Fucking on someone she wasn't supposed to be fucking at all was the only thing that she loved even more. Zyan had surprised her, though. She hadn't expected him to be so vulgar, but she wasn't going to complain.

She liked that shit.

For a few minutes Sulani typed up and deleted a few different replies but none of them seemed suitable enough to describe what she was feeling. It had been three weeks since she had last had sex. She and Dolo had break up sex and she hadn't been with anyone since, deciding to take some time to date and be with herself. She hadn't been the same since her father had passed six months prior, she didn't realize it, but she was still grieving, and it had affected her relationship with Dolo severely. He had been stressing her out and she was in serious need of some stress relief.

Sulani checked the time, it was after one in the morning and the dorm had been locked down for the night. *I could just go in there...*

She bit down on her thumb nail, contemplating rather or not she should go and shoot her shot. It would be nothing for her to slip into the darkened dorm and let herself into Zyan and Pressure's cell. It really was the ideal situation for her because though she wasn't familiar with Zyan, she knew Pressure and she was comfortable around him. He was one of the most solid niggas that she knew and didn't have to worry about him opening his lips about her extracurricular activities. And she trusted the information that her cousin had given her.

Fuck it... She thought and stood up from her desk chair and slipped out of the booth. And into the darkened door.

As quietly as she could, she slipped into the darkened dorm and as quietly as she could, she made her way to the Zyan and Pressure's cell and let herself inside. When she stepped in, Zyan and Pressure were both laying on their cots, looking in her direction. "Wassup, P?" She said and nodded at him.

He smirked at her and nodded back at her. "'Sup, Su."

Sulani met Zyan's eyes next. The lighting in the room was

dim but there was no mistaking the heat that Zyan saw in her eyes. "Zyan."

"Sulani..." He replied and licked his lips, hopping down from his spot in the top bunk. "Thought you was 'bout to ghost a nigga." He spoke taking slow steps toward her.

When he was within arm's reach, Sulani reached her hands up and seductively ran them up his chest. "Now why would I want to do that?" She asked, her voice dripping with lust as she took him in.

"Shit... ain't no tellin'..." Zyan's voice dropped a few octaves, his dick stiffening by the second. He bit down into his bottom lip when he felt her soft hands slip underneath the white wife-beater that he was wearing.

"You straight, P?" Sulani's voice called out to Pressure.

"I'm good, Su. Do you, ma." She could hear the humor in his tone.

Sulani looked up at Zyan from underneath her pretty, long eyelashes. "Tell me..." she hooked both her index fingers into the waistband of his pants and tugged him toward her. "What you say you wanted again?" She questioned him.

Zyan took the opportunity to grab Sulani by the ass and squeezed both of her big ass cheeks. "Some of that pussy." He grunted softly when she slipped one of her tiny hands into his shorts and gripped his hard dick and stroked it.

"And..?" Sulani asked, flicking her tongue out to lick the seam of his lips when he leaned down to kiss her.

"That throat." He groaned and then closed the distance between them, engaging her in a sloppy kiss.

"Mmm." Sulani moaned into Zyan's mouth. The feeling of his thick lips against hers made her melt into him.

Zyan parted her lips with his tongue, his hands busying themselves with pulling her tucked shirt out of her pants and then pulled it over her head, leaving her in her bra. His hands trailed up her soft skin, the smell of sweet jasmine wafting into his nose, making his head swim when he buried his face in the crook of her neck while his hands went to her titties. His warm hands slipped into the cups of her bra, his fingers quickly finding the thick peaks of her nipples.

Sulani moaned softly when he pinched the sensitive buds and dropped her head back as she continued stroking her hard length in her hand. Irritated with the way that the elastic of his waistband restricted her movements, Sulani pushed his shorts down his thighs so that she could free his throbbing dick from his shorts.

Sulani looked at Zyan's thickness and bit her lip then lowered herself to her knees. He was about to open his mouth and speak when Sulani wrapping hers on his dick stopped him. "Damn..." He licked his lips and groaned.

For a few minutes he said nothing. Only the sounds of Sulani sucking and slobbing on his dick mixed with his grunts and groans filled the air. He put one hand on the back of her head, forcing her to take more of his dick down her throat, and put the other behind his head, gripping the back of his neck.

The sounds of her gagging on his meat made him inhale sharply. "Ooh," he licked his lips again, he could feel them going dry, she was sucking him so good. "That's right, gimme that throat."

His words and him shoving his length farther down her throat made Sulani's pussy throb. She could feel herself soaking through her panties, she was so turned on. Overwhelmed with lust, the correctional officer lost herself as she throated the inmate.

"Pretty ass." Zyan shook his head in awe. The last thing he expected was to be fucking any of the C.O.'s but thanks to what seemed to be a fluke, he almost felt like the woman had practically landed in his lap.

Initially when he first met her, he had assumed that she would be hard to get, especially once he had approached her and seemed to be irritated with him. For some reason, she had intrigued him from the moment that he had laid eyes on her when she walked into his cell the day before. He hadn't expected her to give in to his advances so quickly, but he wasn't complaining. If anything, it made him like her even more.

When she looked up at him, he loved the way her long eyelashes fanned daintily against the lids of her pretty, brown, almond shaped eyes. For a moment he felt almost hypnotized as she pleased him with her mouth.

"I want to taste you." He said, removing his hand from the back of her head. "Turn around and bend over."

Sulani stood to her feet, turned and was about to bed over when Zyan grabbing her arm and stepping to the side and pushing her toward Pressure. "Nuh, uh. Face, P. Let my nigga see yo face while I eat this pussy." He demanded.

Sulani bit her lip as her eyes shot over to Pressure who was lounging on his cot, his eyes on the two of them with his dick in hard, beating his own meat. A shiver shook her spine as she took in Pressure's handsome face. A smirk was on his lips as he gave Sulani a knowing look and winked at her.

She smirked back at him as she unbuckled and unbuttoned her pants for Zyan before she placed her hands on the edge of Pressure's bed and bent over, bracing herself for what she knew was coming next.

Zyan dropped to his hunches and tugged her work pants and uniform down her legs until they were puddled around her ankles. With both hands he gripped her ass cheeks and spread them, exposing her sex to him completely. She was soaked, her pussy lips puffy and coated in the evidence of her arousal. The smell emanated from her consumed him with lust and made his thirst for her greater. He wasted not a moment more, licked up her drippage and then stuck his long tongue deep into her center.

He swirled it around the soft walls of her middle, her juices coating his tastebuds and making his dick pulse with need. Zyan pulled his tongue from her center, and he squeezed both her cheeks in his hands as he trailed his tongue down to her clit and circled the sensitive nub with the tip of his tongue.

Overwhelmed with pleasure, Sulani gasped for air, her eyes locked in on Pressure's hand gliding up and down his long length at a steady pace. She couldn't help herself when she laid her face on his stomach while she did her best to catch her breath, but it was difficult to do when Zyan lapping at her pussy deliciously. "Oh fuck!" She moaned, her eyes rolling in the back of her head when he sucked her clit into his mouth.

Once his thirst was quenched, Zyan slapped Sulani on the ass and then stood to his feet. He pulled Sulani to him by her hips and licked his lips as he lined the head of his dick up with the entrance of her pussy. Momentarily, he thought about asking if she had a condom, but just as quickly as it came, it left when Sulani reached a warm hand between her thighs to massage his balls while he teased her pussyhole with the head of his dick. *Fuck it...* was his attitude. He had already ate the bitch out. If she had some shit, he already had it.

"Zyaaan." Sulani whimpered his name when he put her out of her misery and filled her. It was in that moment that she realized how sexually pent up she was when her body melted at the feel of him entering her. Her entire body relaxed, and she arched her back. She folded her arms over Pressure's stomach and rested her head on her folded arms. "Fuck, I needed thisss." She whimpered in pleasure.

"Damn, this muthafucka grippin'." Zyan moaned, pulling out if her and slapping his dick against her clit. She already had him on the verge of nutting. He didn't know if it was because it had been some months since he last had some pussy, if it he was wildly attracted to her, or if the coochie was just that good. Either way, he was far from ready for it to be over.

Sulani's moans were soft, she didn't want to make too much noise and draw unnecessary attention to them. Pressure took one of her hands and wrapped it around his dick and she didn't hesitate to stroke his length for him while Zyan slid his hardness back into her ocean, raw dick and all. Her eyes rolled into the back of her head as his dick touched places inside her pussy that she had no clue even existed. One hand was gripping a hand full of her ass, pulling her back against him so that he could stroke even deeper into her.

"You feel so good." The sounds that were coming from her reminded Zyan of a cat purring. There was a different kind of energy about her that pleasantly turned him on. Maybe it was the sounds that she was making, or it could have been the mischievous quality to her. All he knew was that there was a wild nature to her that he could sense. It made him want to tame her. Domesticate her.

Zyan was thoroughly enjoying hitting Sulani from the back. He found himself turned on even more as he watched her jack his best friend off while he fucked her. Had it been any other nigga, he wouldn't have let the shit fly, but he and Pressure were like brothers. The way that he saw it, Pressure was more like a brother to him than his own *twin* brother was. "Suck it." He slapped her on the ass.

It wouldn't have been the first time they slutted a woman out together. That wasn't anything new for them.

Zyan shook his head in blissful disbelief, he hadn't known what he did to deserve such a treat, but he was grateful.

Sulani took Pressure's dick into her and moaned at the taste of him on her tongue. She gently sucked on the head and soft moans fell from her lips with each of Zyan's thrusts. A hard thrust caused Pressure's dick to slide farther into her mouth, his long length hitting the back of her throat with each thrust.

"Look at them sexy ass lips wrapped around my dick." Pressure sighed, content and put his hand on the back of her head, guiding her movements to take his dick deeper and deeper down her throat while she gagged on it.

Sulani moaned around Pressure's dick when Zyan slipped a hand between her thighs and toyed with her clit while steadily stroking his thickness in and out of her. Her pussy was soaked, causing Zyan to slip effortlessly in and out of her center.

Zyan bit hard into his lip, his eyes squeezed shut. He was close. "Fuck!" he cursed, quickly pulled out and shot his load all over Sulani's ass.

Pressure groaned, his dick throbbing hard, a signal of his own orgasm approaching. Sulani felt the hard throb and pulled him out of her mouth just as he erupted and instead rubbed the head of his dick and his cum all over her lips, humming her approval.

The sound of all three of them breathlessly laughing filled the cell in between heavy pants as they all busied themselves with cleaning up and getting back dressed.

"Good shit, boys... Whew," Sulani rested her hands on her hips after she finished dressing again. A big grin stretched across her face, and she felt energized. "I needed that. Bad..." She shook her head at the realization.

Pressure laid on his bed, a lazy grin on his face and both his arms behind his head. Zyan was sitting on the floor, leaning up against the back wall. "Same." He said, cooly.

Zyan nodded in agreement. "Yeah... I did, too."

"Alrighty, fellas... I'll catch you guys' layer... Y'all be smoove." She said, and then quietly slipped out of them men's cell and made her way back to her designated spot in the booth. Her mental fog had cleared, and her spirit felt lighter.

With a smile on her face, Sulani picked up her book and enjoyed the rest of her easy shift.

Chapter 3

"Aye, P, how you know Sulani?" Zyan asked Pressure the following morning.

Pressure chuckled. "Gemini is her cousin." He stated simply.

Zyan burst out laughing. "I don't know how, but that shit makes sense. I always knew her ass came from a family of freaks."

Zyan had met Pressure through Gemini. When Zyan was seventeen, he and McKenzie had gone to a house party and when the young couple was leaving, they had left out of the back door and found a passed-out Gemini laying on the side of the house battered, bleeding, and left for dead. The couple picked the woman up, took her to the hospital and stuck around to make sure that she was okay.

McKenzie and Gemini had been best friends ever since. Pressure was her boyfriend, so naturally, because the women were practically joined at the hip, Zyan and Pressure had become just as close. The four of them had a bond that had withstood many tests. In many ways they were all indebted to one another. They were a family.

Though Zyan was very familiar with Gemini, he didn't know much about her biological family. It was a sensitive subject for her, so he didn't mention it. What he did know about her was that they were wealthy and well-connected. To find that Sulani was related to Gemini piqued his interest in her even more.

Gemini was good people, so he was interested to see what Sulani was about.

"That's how you was able to get her to bring you that pack?" Zyan asked. He was laying on his bed, his phone resting on his stomach as he scrolled through Instagram mindlessly.

"Kinda. It was really her idea. I knew she was a C.O. but I didn't know she worked at this prison. Sulani is really the only person in her family that Gem talks to. She's hella coo, though. Met her a couple times. Remember when we needed to find out where that nigga Da'vion was at least year? Su was the one who found him for us." Pressure enlightened Zyan. "Su hit Gem and asked her if I needed anything and that she could bring it to me and she made it happen. She fronted me the work, too. Just had me pay her to make the drop."

Zyan nodded to himself, listening intently. "Damn, why you ain't say nothin and ask a nigga if he needed anything?" He asked in reference to himself.

"Maaan, I leave yo ass alone when you get to goin' through it with Kenzie, bro. Y'all be stressin' me the fuck out just havin' to listen to y'all asses. I was stayin' out the way."

Zyan said nothing, his irritation peaking at the thought of McKenzie. He hadn't been liking her attitude as of late and that was something that bothered him even more. McKenzie had always been there to hold him down since the day that he had met her.

He was sixteen when his mom and stepfather kicked him out of the house with nothing but the clothes on his back.

It was three in the morning, and it was dark outside on the streets of Stockton, California. Tears streamed were streaming down his face, the cold and bitter early January air drying them almost just as fast as they fell. The teenage didn't do too much crying throughout his life. He had been programed to believe that it wasn't okay for a man to cry. It had made him a hard man, but every once in a while, the pain that he felt in his heart would be so great that he couldn't help but to. When he did, it was always when he was alone.

He had been roaming through the streets for hours. The thick hood of his black sweater was pulled tight around his head, the black beanie he was wearing giving his head an extra layer of protection and warmth from the air. His hands were tucked into the pocket of his designer jeans, and then Jay's on his feet looked to be new.

His mind was reeling, replaying the nights events.

"I can't do this no more, Zyan. You gotta go..."

He shook his head, shaking off the memory, but her words kept repeating in his head over and over again.

"She really picked that nigga over me..." He mumbled to himself, his tears falling even faster.

He had gotten into a physical fight with his stepfather that night and after it was all said and done, Zyan had beat the man so bad that his mother kicked her own son out of the family home. The house that his biological father had built for his family from the ground up.

The hurt that Zyan felt was beyond anything that she could have ever imagined. What hurt him is that it only confirmed what he had been feeling since he was a young child. That his mother didn't love him.

He had come to her defense and like she always did, she had picked her husband over her son. Nothing hurt Zyan more than his mother's rejection.

He was walking through a random park. On the other side of the park, he saw a set of benches and tables and decided that he would sleep there for the night. He was tired from walking for hours. His feet were aching, and he had a headache, he needed to rest.

As he got closer to the benches, the sound of someone's soft and feminine moans could be heard. Alert, Zyan's eyes carefully scanned the area until he came could make out the silhouette of what he could tell was a girl bent over. One of her hands was braced against the grass and though he couldn't see the other hand, he assumed that she was either holding her dress up, or her ass cheeks apart. It was clear what she was doing.

Deciding to mind his business, Zyan made his way to the benches and sat down. He groaned when he stretched his legs out and flexed his feet, wincing at the throbbing of his feet once he got his weight off them.

"Uggghh," A load groan came from behind the tree. It was about ten feet away.

Zyan chuckled to himself. He found it to be amusing. It was such a random for him witness.

Moments later, he could hear the two talking but he couldn't make out what they were saying.

"Nigga, fuck you, I ain't givin' you shit back! You wanted to fuck, you gave me a hunnit dollas and I gave you what you wanted! Ain't my fuckin' fault you nutted quick!"

The female shouting made Zyan's head snap in their direction. He could see the silhouettes of two people. One towered over the other, the shorter of the two obviously a female and the taller one male. The female was walking backwards cautiously.

"Bitch, you gon' gimme my mufuckin' money back!" The man charged at her.

She tried to run but she wasn't fast enough, and he grabbed the strap of her purse and attempted to snatch it from her. She had been expected him to do so and had grabbed the mace that she had hooked to the bag and sprayed him in the face.

The man clutched at his face, but hung on to the strap, and they proceeded to have a tug of war match. Before he could stop himself, Zyan was running over there and punched the man in the jaw, sending him and the female to the floor when he didn't let go of the purse strap. When Zyan saw he hadn't let go of the bag yet, he stomped on his hand making the man yelp in pain.

As soon as he let go, she pulled the bag from within' his reach and rolled away from him before standing up. She watched Zyan rummage through the man's pockets while he rolled around, clutching his hand in pain.

"Bitch ass nigga," Zyan spat, counting the loose bills that were crumbled up in his pocket. "If you paid for the pussy then you paid for the pussy, nigga. The fuck?"

He turned away and looked at the female. He couldn't see her well in the dark, but he could see her well enough to know that she was attractive. She had on nothing but a crop top, a mini-skirt, and some flip flops. "You good?" He asked and gestured with his head for them to start walking.

She glanced at the man still on the floor and nodded, following her hero's lead. "Yeah, I'm good. Thank you."

They were quiet for a few minutes as they followed the concrete pathway out of the park. "Where you going?" Zyan asked after a while. By then they were standing on the side-walk of the park, standing under an orange streetlight and he could see her more clearly.

Though her face was painted in makeup, he could tell that the girl was young, maybe eighteen or nineteen. Young, but old enough. He assumed she was older than him. She was very pretty in the face, and she was what most guys his age called slim thick. He could see why the nigga had chucked up the money to get a feel of her insides.

She sighed. "It's a motel up the street." She opened up her purse and pulled the money that she had made that night out and began counting it. "I'm still forty short for a room tonight, though. Fuck..."

Zyan heard the raw emotion in her voice and could tell she felt like crying. He felt for her. He also had a rough night. He watched the young woman fold her arms across her chest as she began shivering. He took his sweater off, leaving him in the white T-shirt that he had on underneath, he still had on more clothing than she did, so he handed her the sweater. Then he dug in his pocket and pulled out the sixty dollars that he had taken off the trick, counted out forty and held it out to her. "Here, there go the other forty. I'll walk you there."

The girl gave him a stare, her bottom lip trembling with

gratitude. She had had a long day and was thanked God for sending someone to show her some grace. "Thank you." She said and slipped the oversized sweater over her head.

Forty minutes later, the pair made it to the entrance of the Motel 6. Zyan stood outside and waited for the girl to get her room. When she came back outside, she leaned against the wall next to him just as he was.

"You get your room?" He asked.

"Nah, not yet. I'm gonna wait till after checkout. If I get it now, I'll have to leave at checkout still. It's already seven," she looked out at the morning sky. The sun had risen, a clear indicator of a new day. She had spent nearly all night out in the cold, slanging pussy for money to get somewhere to lay her head.

Zyan said nothing but nodded his head.

The female cleared her throat. "Um, I don't know what you have going on, but um... A double bed is a little cheaper than I thought, and since you gave me the rest of what I needed... and since you helped me out... We could share the room if you want. There's a Denny's across the street, we can go sit in there and eat until check-in." She turned and looked at Zyan.

He met her eyes, contemplating her offer.

"Plus, you don't look that much older than me... I'd doubt you'd be able to get a room on your own." She didn't know if he was homeless or not, but she figured he had nowhere to go, because why else would he be wandering through a dark park in the early morning hours in the cold.

Zyan raised his eyebrows. "How old are you?"

"Sixteen..." She said sheepishly.

Zyan looked at her shocked. She looked older than that. "So how you able to get a room?"

She shrugged. "I know someone here."

Zyan went quiet and just stared at the girl for a few minutes. He had no other options. She seemed harmless enough and just as he had helped her out, she had helped him out.

So, he agreed. "Okay, coo..."

THE TWO OF them had been together ever since.

Together they had got it out of the mud, hustling in every way that they could to survive and thrive. That's why her distance hurt Zyan so much. He and McKenzie had survived things that should have broken them and their bond, and yet she had still been there by his side.

The last thing he wanted was for his brother and his prison bid to be the thing that broke them, but his faith was small. McKenzie was switching up on him and he didn't know how he could take that.

"Yeah, aiight." Zyan mumbled after a while. "Thanks for the insight." He thanked his friend.

"Zyan..."

"Hm?"

"Ease up on Kenz, man. That girl loves you. You know she do. You got her doing a lot. Don't push her away, or yo ass gon' be sick once she decides to move on with her life." McKenzie was like a sister to him. While he stayed out of their business, he was always one to be honest and let his friend know when he was wrong.

That was something that Zyan appreciated about Pressure. He let him know when he was wrong, but always said it in a way that let him know that he wasn't judging him for it. He received criticism.

Zyan sighed, "Yeah, bro... I'ma chill." He couldn't deny that his friend had a point. He knew that she was only doing what he had asked her to. It was just his insecurity speaking. There was a part of him that had already understood that. There was an insecurity that he had yet to address within' himself.

McKenzie dealing with his twin brother Zyair intimidated him more than he was willing to admit. Zyan was aware that Zyair possessed everything that McKenzie would need from a man. She would miss out on nothing by choosing to be with Zyair instead of him.

That would cut him deeper than he could have imagined. The thought of that was something that Zyan couldn't bear.

He had to stay out of his head and busy himself with something else rather than obsessing about what McKenzie and his brother could have been doing. His mind couldn't help but wonder each time he thought of them together. His fire was only fueled whenever she missed his calls or took too long to text him back.

I need a distraction.

Just as he had thought, a message with an attachment came through from Sulani, and he quickly opened it. It was a picture of her pussy, her phat life puffy, and her clit erect and peeking from under its hood.

Sulani: My pussy and throat still sore lol...

Zyan bit his lip to hide his smile. It was just the distraction that he needed.

"Aye, you ever fuck wit' Sulani? How you think Gemini would feel about that?" He was curious now that he knew the two women were cousins.

Pressure laughed. Zyan imagined that he was grinning. "Shiiit... they cousins that's all I'ma say." He laughed even harder.

"Aw hell nah!" Zyan jumped down from his bed and looked at Pressure. He was grinning. "What that mean?"

"Gon' man, it don't mean nothin'." He waved him off but couldn't stop chuckling."

"They be fuckin' with each other?!"

"If you don't get yo freaky ass on, nah, bruh. Ain't none of that goin' on." Pressure shook his head while chuckling. "You somethin' else."

"Whatever, nigga." He laughed and went to take a leak. "They ever kiss at least?" He asked a few minutes later.

"Shut the fuck up, bruh." Pressure roared with laughter.

A FEW HOURS LATER, Zyan and Pressure were coming in from the yard when three C.O.'s walked up on them.

"You two, turn around and put your hands behind your back, you comin' wit' me." One of them said.

Zyan screwed his face up at the purple muthafucka. "Fo' what?"

The swole officer pulled his taser from his pocket and pointed it at him. "Do what I said inmate?"

Pressure sucked his teeth. "Man, y'all on some bullshit, what we do?" He turned and did as they said. "Come on, bruh, let's not even give these muthafuckas a reason to do no bull-shit, bro. It's good." He tried to reason with Zyan. He knew his brother enough to know he'd buck on them just for fucking with him for no reason. He needed to keep him calm.

Zyan mumbled something under his breath but followed in Pressure's actions and did as the officer's said. The officers lead them to the back of the prison in the staff parking lot.

"The fuck we doin' back here?!" Zyan asked in irritation as the purple muthafucka took his handcuffs off of he and Pressure and they stood side by side, staring at the three offi-cers glaring at them.

One of them was a fat ass black dude that was breathing hard as he stood to the left of the purple man. His bald head seemed too small for his body, and he had big ass bifocal glasses being held up by his big ears and nose. His belly was big, and his legs were little. The other officer was the shortest of all the men, was lanky and had twists in his head.

"I hear you been talkin' to my girl inmate..." Purple Man said pulling a pair of fingerless gloves onto his hands.

Zyan and Pressure stared blankly at the nigga for a few moments, then looked at each other, then back at the officers and burst out laughing at the same time.

"This blurple gorilla face ass mufucka really serious!" Zyan put his hand on Pressure's shoulder and pointed at the officer with his thumb.

Pressure had his hands on his knees while he laughed. "Aye, he brought back up! His security look hella hard! We so scared!"

They both laughed even louder.

"Oh shit!" Zyan laughed and leaned back, dodging the left hook the Purple Man threw at him when he rushed forward to attack Zyan. "Mink!" He said as he threw a punch of his own, connecting with Dolo's chin.

"Damn, Dolo! Get that nigga!" The fat officer huffed.

Dolo grunted in dismay and squared up with the inmate. "Come on fucker! Don't run!"

"What?! Let's squab then, nigga!" Zyan pulled his pants up and squared back up with him.

Dolo moved in and threw two punches, he missed the first one, and the second one connected with the left side of Zyan's ribs. The punch hurt and made Zyan wince, but he kept it moving, hitting him right back with two powerful punches of his own. "Mink! Mink!" One hit him in the eye, the other in his neck. The neck punch made Dolo gag and bite down hard on his tongue.

From the sidelines, Pressure was laughing his ass off when he heard the audible gag. He had never seen a nigga get punched in the throat like that before. He couldn't imagine going out like that. "Whew shit! This shit so goddamn funny!" His stomach was hurting.

"Come on! You wanted this right?" Zyan egged Dolo on. "Pussy ass nigga wanna fight over a bitch. Got me fucked up! Boop!" He jumped forward and socked Dolo against the temple.

The officer hit the floor, falling like a tower.

"Stop fuckin' playin' with me, bit–" before he could finish his sentence, he felt something hard hit him in the back of the head. "Ah!"

The fat officer had rushed to Dolo's aid and bapped Zyan on the head with his baton. Pressure's laugh grew louder. He knew he needed to help his friend, but the moment was so ridiculous that he couldn't help but laugh. Zyan couldn't see the way the officer looked holding up his pants that were sliding off of his too little legs because his belt wasn't secured around his big belly sufficiently.

After regaining his composure, Pressure ran up to the fat officer who was repeatedly beating Zyan with the baton and pushed him over, sending him rolling like a rollie polie across the parking lot. He had just turned to look for the third officer, Pressure was tazed, sending him dropping to the ground.

"We about to be in some deep shit..." The third officer sighed looking at both Zyan and Pressure passed out in the parking lot and his fellow officers struggling to pick themselves up off the floor.

Chapter 4

Zyan: I fought your boyfriend today

Sulani: He's not my boyfriend, but yeah, I heard about that... I'm sorry that happened to you. That nigga be trippin' smh...

Sulani: Are you okay?

Zyan: I'm straight. I do got a crazy headache, though...

Sulani: I wish I could make it go away...

Zyan: Let me see you...

Sulani: What you mean?

Zyan: I want to video call you.

Sulani: How we do that?

Zyan: You got Instagram?

Sulani: No.

Zyan: Facebook?

Sulani: No.

Zyan: Snapchat?

Sulani: No...

Zyan: Damn, do you have any social media? What do you have?

Sulani: Lol I don't do social media. I be having too much going on, ya know?

Zyan: I feel you. Just a sec...

After the fight, the officers woke the two inmates up and walked them back to their cells and ignored their requests to go to medical. They had no intentions of reporting the incident and he was sure that they were going to try to cover up their tracks.

Moments later, Sulani's phone rang. "Hello," she answered.

"That hella sucks you ain't got no way for me to video call you, but I guess just your voice will suffice. Whatchu doin'?" Zyan's deep baritone hit her right between the legs.

"I'm just chillin' watchin' TV, right now. Are you okay?" She asked. She had gotten a copy of the video footage from the back parking lot. Word had traveled around the compound fast and like he always did, Dolo was embarrassing the fuck out of her at her job.

"I'm fine. You needa be asking your nigga that." He said arrogantly.

"I told you he wasn't my boyfriend. I *used* to fuck around with him, but that nigga too jealous and doesn't understand what no means. I moved to working that dorm to get away from his ass. He wanna fight any nigga I even *look* at too long. He's toxic as fuck." She sounded exasperated. "That nigga stresses me out."

"I can imagine so... I get it, though... that pussy *good*." Zyan chuckled.

"I meaaan it's not my fault I got that supa soaka." Her voice got high, making it sound seductive. "That dick was hittin', too. I ain't even get to finish, but I ain't have *no* complaints. I enjoyed myself." Her voice sounded like a purr.

"Yeah?" His voice was husky, his dick growing hard as he recalled their first session. "You enjoy suck my nigga off, too?" He questioned.

"Yeah, I did, actually. I know you felt it when it made me wetter."

"I did. You a nasty hoe. I know yo type." He couldn't help but to start fisting his erection. The turn in conversation aroused him.

Sulani giggled, "I know you do. Like attracts like, right? I know I'm your type."

"You callin' me a hoe?"

"I might be. Birds of a feather, right?" She chuckled.

"Whatchu mean?" She had thrown him for a loop. He didn't know what she meant by that.

"Ain't yo girl a hoe?"

Zyan didn't say anything.

"My cousin is a hoe... And Pressure's ass a hoe, too. So, yeah... birds of a feather." She doubled down on her stance.

"Speaking of Pressure..." He spoke more loudly to get his celly's attention. "You was real comfortable suckin' him off last night. That you just enjoying yourself being a hoe or what?"

She laughed at his question while reading between the lines. "What he tell you when you asked him about it."

"He ain't tell me shit, that's why I'm asking you." He chuckled.

"I know he didn't," she said smugly. "That's my dawg. I was just doing him a favor." She said as if it was nothing.

"That's the kind of friend you are, huh? That make me one of your friends?"

"Nah, you are more like one of my *thingies.*"

"Aw hell nah! Don't make my dick go soft, girl. The fuck is a thingy?" He couldn't help but to laugh at her silliness.

"I'm just playin'. But nah, for real, though... We don't even have to do all that. You wanted some pussy. I wanted some dick. And we both got what we wanted. What's wrong with that?"

"Nothin' at all." He mumbled huskily, his dick throbbing hard in his hand. "I like you, Sulani."

"Aw, how cute." She cooed.

"When you gon let a nigga get some more of that?"

Sulani laughed. "That fight ain't slow you down, huh?"

"Hell, nah, ain't nobody worried bout that bitch ass nigga," he said dismissively.

"If you say so. I'm off the next two nights. We'll see what happens."

"Make me cum, Su. Moan for me." Zyan sucked in air between his feet and grunted, feeling himself getting close to his peak.

"Ooh," she moaned sensually into the phone, making his imagination run wild. It was just enough to send him over the edge and make him cum.

THE MOON HUNG low in the sky, casting a pale light through the thin curtains of Sulani's living room. The digital clock on her mantle read 2:33 AM, and the world outside was silent except for the occasional rustle of wind through the trees. She had just settled into the deep embrace of her couch, wrapped in a blanket, a book laid open on her lap as her eyelids grew heavy.

Suddenly, a sharp rattle at the front door jolted her from her drowsiness. Her heart began to race as the rattle grew into a series of heavy thuds. Sulani set her book aside and cautiously moved toward the noise, the floorboards creaking under her weight.

"Who's there?" she called out, recognizing the familiar pattern of persistence.

The door burst open, and Dolo stumbled into the apartment, his eyes glazed and unfocused. The smell of alcohol enveloped the room like a toxic cloud.

"Sulani, we need to talk," he slurred, his voice echoing against the walls.

She took a step back, her heart pounding. "Darius, you're drunk. You can't just break into my house like this. You need to leave."

But he wasn't listening. His bloodshot eyes fixed on her, filled with a volatile mix of anger and desperation. He advanced; his steps unsteady.

"I just want us to go back to the way things were," he pleaded, reaching out toward her.

Sulani's mind raced. She had taken self-defense classes after their breakup, and the instructors' voices echoed in her head: *Stay calm. Keep your distance. Be assertive.*

"Darius, please stop. You're scaring me. You need to leave now," she demanded, trying to keep her voice steady.

He continued to advance, his expression turning angry. "You can't just throw me out of your life, Su!" he shouted, his voice slurring.

Sulani's back hit the wall behind her, her escape route cut off. Adrenaline surged through her veins as she braced herself. When Dolo reached out to grab her, she ducked under his arm and darted past him, heading for the phone in the kitchen.

Dolo, however, was quicker than she anticipated in his

drunken state. He grabbed her arm, spinning her around. "You're not calling anyone!" he yelled, his grip tightening.

Instinctively, Sulani's self-defense training kicked in. She twisted her arm in the way she had been taught, breaking his grip, and followed it with a swift elbow to his stomach. Dolo doubled over, but he was relentless. He lunged at her again, and this time they both crashed to the ground in a tangle of limbs.

The fight was chaotic. Sulani fought with every ounce of her strength, trying to push Dolo off her. He was heavy and aggressive, but the alcohol made him clumsy. They rolled across the floor, knocking over furniture and sending items from the coffee table skittering across the room.

Then, her hand brushed against something cold and hard on the floor. It was a small decorative knife—a gift from a friend that she kept on the coffee table. Her heart skipped a beat. She knew she couldn't let Dolo get the weapon.

Seizing the knife, Sulani managed to free herself and scramble to her feet, holding the knife out in front of her defensively. "Dolo, stop! I don't want to hurt you!" she exclaimed, her voice trembling but firm.

Dolo, clutching his stomach, glared at her with a mix of shock and rage. "You're going to stab me?" he spat, a wild look in his eyes.

Sulani's mind was racing. She didn't want to use the knife; she didn't even want it in her hands. It was a symbol of how far things had spiraled out of control. "No, I don't want to stab you, but I will defend myself," she said, backing towards the front door, hoping she could edge around him and escape.

He took a step forward, and Sulani tightened her grip on the knife. "I'm not going to let you leave me, Su," he said, his voice a mix of a threat and a plea.

Dolo's back hit the front door. She reached behind her, fumbling for the doorknob. "You don't get to decide that, Dolo. It's over," she stated, her voice gaining strength from her resolve.

He lunged for her again, but this time Sulani was prepared. She sidestepped, and as he stumbled past her, she opened the door and bolted outside, the knife still in her hand.

The cool night air hit her like a splash of water to the face. She didn't stop to look back as she ran barefoot across her apartment complex. She pounded on one of her neighbor's doors, glancing over her shoulder to see if Dolo had followed.

The door opened, and her neighbor—an older woman named Diane—appeared, her eyes wide with concern. "Sulani, what on earth—"

"Please, call the police," Sulani gasped, out of breath and shaking. "It's Darius. He's in my house."

Diane pulled Sulani inside and locked the door behind them. While Diane dialed 911, Sulani collapsed to the floor, the knife clattering beside her. She wrapped her arms around herself, trying to shake the image of the anger in Dolo's eyes.

Within minutes, the flashing lights of police cars lit up the street. Officers entered Sulani's apartment, and after what felt like an eternity, they emerged with Darius in handcuffs. He didn't resist; the fight seemed to have left him as quickly as it had come.

Sulani gave her statement to the police, her hands still trembling. Diane stayed by her side, offering silent support. As the officers led Dolo to a squad car, he turned to look at Sulani. There was no anger in his eyes now, only a hollow sadness.

Sulani watched the car drive away, a new sense of relief washing over her. The night's events had shattered the quiet of her home, but she knew she had done what she needed to do to protect herself.

In the days that followed, Sulani would have to deal with the aftermath of the break-in and the fight. She would need to mend the broken pieces, both in her home and within herself. But she had faced her fear, and in doing so, she had found a reservoir of strength she hadn't known she possessed.

That night, as Sulani finally returned to her own bed, the knife safely in the hands of the police, she realized that she had survived. And while the road to recovery would be long and undoubtedly difficult, she felt a spark of hope that with time, she would heal.

The next morning, the sunlight streamed through the windows, illuminating the disarray from the night before. The overturned furniture, the scattered items, and the broken vase on the floor were stark reminders of the struggle. As she surveyed the damage, Sulani knew the physical cleanup was just the beginning.

She made a mental list of what needed to be done. The lock on the front door would have to be changed. Her home, once her sanctuary, now felt vulnerable and exposed. She would call a locksmith later that day.

As the initial shock began to fade, Sulani considered reaching out for support. She knew that the emotional and psychological impact of last night's confrontation would linger far longer than the bruises that were beginning to form on her arms and legs. She made a note to look for a counselor or a support group for people who had been through similar experiences. She didn't have to go through this alone.

Sulani spent the morning cleaning up the physical remnants of the night's events. With each item she righted, each shard of glass she swept up, she felt as though she was slowly reclaiming her space. It was a small act of defiance against the chaos that Dolo had tried to bring into her life.

In the following days, Sulani took steps to fortify her sense of security. She installed a new security system with cameras that she could monitor from her phone. The locksmith strengthened the locks on her doors and windows. Her neighbors, especially Diane, kept a watchful eye on her home, and the community rallied around her, offering support and assistance.

Dolo was charged with breaking and entering, assault, and

attempted assault with a deadly weapon. He was given a restraining order, barring him from coming near Sulani or attempting to contact her. It was not a victory—there was no triumph in the pain that had been caused—but it was a step toward closure.

The night that Dolo broke into her home had been the most terrifying of her life, but it had also been a turning point. Sulani had faced her deepest fears, fought back, and emerged with a newfound determination to live her life on her own terms.

"Damn, Su, what happened?" Zyan asked, waiting for Sulani tell him about what had transpired between she and her ex. She was at home, relaxing in her bed video chatting Zyan. She had taken some time off work to process what she experienced with Dolo.

That night, there was a weight on her heart, a piece of her story that she had yet to share with him.

"Dolo broke into my house while he was drunk." Sulani sighed and paused, the memories vivid and sharp. "He wanted to get back together, but when I refused, things got crazy."

Zyan shook his head in disbelief, a protective instinct flaring in his eyes. "That must have been scary," he said, his voice low and steady.

"It was," Sulani admitted. "But I had taken some self-defense classes, and I was able to fight him off until I could get to my neighbor's house and call the police."

As she spoke, Sulani could feel the old fear and adrenaline coursing through her once more, she'd been traumatized. "I'm not going to lie; it was a bit of a wakeup call."

"But you're here now, talking to me about it," Zyan said, his voice full of admiration. "That counts for something, right?"

Sulani gave a small, wry smile. "Right. I knew I couldn't let that night define the rest of my life. I think I'ma go to therapy to help find a sense of security again. This shit has made me paranoid."

Zyan looked into the camera, his eyes never leaving her face. "And what about love? Has that experience changed how you feel about opening your heart again?"

The question hung in the air, and Sulani felt the weight of her past brush against the possibility of a future with Zyan. "For a long time, I was scared," she confessed. "Scared of being vulnerable, scared of trusting someone new. But I've come to realize that what happened with Dolo was about him and his issues, not about my worth or my ability to love and be loved."

"I refuse to let that one night stop me from finding happiness. It would be like letting him win, and I won't do that. I won't let fear dictate my life."

Zyan's expression was one of deep respect as he listened.

"You're strong, Su," he said softly. "And for what it's worth, I'm here for you, at whatever pace you need to go."

Sulani's heart fluttered at his words, at the understanding and patience that shone through. "Thank you. That means more to me than you know. I want to move forward, and I know that one day I will. But I also need you to know that sometimes I might get scared, I might need a little more reassurance.

"I'm here for your, girl." Zyan said, one corner of his mouth pulling up in a half smile.

She smiled back, a genuine, heartfelt smile that lit up her eyes. "I'm not looking for a hero, you know. I've learned that I can be my own. But having someone, a partner, who understands and supports me, that's something I didn't know if I'd find again. Shit, that's something I realize I never had."

"Then let's not think of it as you finding a partner, but rather as us finding each other," he said. "We can be there for one another, to support, to listen, and to grow together. I'm not going anywhere, Sulani. I want to be part of your journey, no matter what it brings. I really fuck witchu."

That warmed Sulani's heart.

As they continued to talk, the conversation moving from heavy to light and back again, Sulani felt a connection to Zyan that went beyond the superficial. Here was someone who saw her not as a victim or a project to fix, but as a person of strength. Someone who was willing to walk beside her, to face the challenges and celebrate the victories, no matter how big or small.

When they finally said their goodbyes and ended their video call, Sulani felt a sense of contentment she hadn't known in a long time.

Chapter 5

"Fuck, baby. I'm finna nut." Zyan groaned lowly, trying to keep his voice down as he blew his large load all over his girlfriend's pretty face. His dick twitched multiple times as she slapped his thickness across her big juicy lips.

"Mmmmm. So good." She mumbled around his dick as she continued to suck him dry.

"Yeah, hoe. Suck the fuck outta that dick." Pressure grunted.

Sulani was on her knees, both Pressure and Zyan towering over her, and she took turns sucking them off. Alternating between sucking and stroking each of them. She gripped Zyan's dick in one hand, and Pressure's in the other. Her soft hands stroking their dicks felt great. Neither of them couldn't wait to fill her.

Her Dolo situation had been resolved. The man had been fired from the job and had given up trying to be with Sulani, allowing herself to move on with her life.

"Stand up." Zyan demanded her and instructed her to bend over. He lined his dick up with her entrance and slowly began to slide inside of her tight pussy. He groaned when he began slipping in with ease, her wet pussy immediately sucking his thickness. "Oh, shit." He moaned. He hadn't been expecting her pussy to be as wet as it was.

Sulani moaned as Pressure continued fucking her face, as she got her pussy pounded by Zyan. She was in complete bliss as she got dug out and her throat fucked. She was being used by two fine ass men and she was loving every second of it.

"Oh, bitch, you got some good ass pussy, I'm 'bout to cum." Zyan groaned, doing his best to hold back his nut. He didn't wanna cum yet, but her pussy was tight, wet, and was inviting as fuck. Her lil shit was milking his dick and it was hands down the best pussy that he had ever had.

Zyan didn't even bother pulling out, choosing instead to cum deep inside of Sulani's good coochie. Filling her up with a huge load of his seed. He was out of breath when he pulled out of her, her pussy immediately leaking with his cum.

Zyan immediately traded places with Pressure and stuck his cum covered dick into her Sulani's mouth, making her suck his semi-hard dick clean. His eyes rolled into the back of his head as her warm mouth sucked him back to a full erection.

"On the bed, turn around and toot that ass up." Pressure demanded as he stroked his dick, waiting for her to get into position.

She released Zyan's dick from her mouth and did as he instructed. The moment that she was on her hands and knees, hands were all over her. Zyan settled himself on the bed underneath her so that he could lay on his back and suck on her hard nipples while Pressure gripped her by the back of her head and pulled it back, making her look up at him while he roughly slapped his dick across her face, repeatedly.

A gasp left her lips when she felt her ass cheeks being spread wide and Pressure spitting into her asshole before licking it and fucking her tight hole with his tongue. She moaned uncontrollably, trying her best to throw her ass back against his face, but he slapped her hard on the ass. "Don't chu fuckin' move." He demanded, then went back to fucking her with his tongue.

"You a nasty ass bitch lettin' me and my nigga slut yo ass out." Zyan said and firmly slapped her across the face. His dick jumped when she moaned in pleasure. He liked that she was liking being used and abused.

He couldn't count how many times he had tried to get McKenzie to let him gang her with his boys. He had a thing for hoes and sharing his bitches with his nigga, but for some odd ass reason, she would always make an excuse about why she wasn't with having a train ran on her. He didn't push it though. What one bitch wouldn't do, another would do that and so much more.

"Mmm, I wanna get in that ass. Open up for me." Pressure said as he stood up and pressed the head of his dick to her asshole and began applying pressure.

Sulani winced in pain as his thickness began stretching her tight hole open. Zyan noticed her pain and reached a hand between her thighs and began toying with her sensitive clit, giving her a subtle distraction from the pain of her ass.

"Good hoe." Pressure cooed, jiggling her fat ass on his dick. "Ooou, this ass so mufuckin' tight." He feed her his dick inch by inch, spitting in it when necessary.

Sulani groaned, her eyes rolling into the back of her head as her body went into sensory overload. There was so much going on and so many different sensations that she was experiencing at once that it sent her over the edge as she came so hard that she passed out.

When she came to, she was sandwiched between the two men. She laid straddling Zyan as he laid beneath her, his thick dick stretching her pussy wide as she creamed all over it. Pressure was behind her, his dick deep in her ass. He had her gripped by her hair, using it to pull her hard onto his and Zyan's dicks.

Sulani whimpered in pleasure when she was realized that she was still being fucked by her cousin's man and his homeboy. It was a dream come true.

"Goddamn, you so fuckin' nasty." Zyan sat up and whispered into her ear before pulling her face to his, wrapping his hand around her neck and sticking his tongue into her mouth in a sloppy wet ass kiss. His dick throbbed hard. He was about to fucking cum.

Pressure pounded into her ass even harder. Zyan's groans and the way he thrusted wildly in and out of her from below let him know that his friend was just as close. A few pumps later, and they both let out loud groans as they both erupted, filling the lil bitch up with nut.

Sulani bit her lip, loving the feel of hot cum dripping out of her ass and pussy. She had been deliciously fucked and she loved every minute of it.

"Thanks for the fun, fellas." Sulani giggled after they all got dressed. She had never been double penetrated before, but it had been amazing. "I'm off for the next two nights, so y'all will have to keep busy until then." She said.

"Yup!" Zyan huffed, already laying on his bed, spent.

"Aight, enjoy yo time off, Su." Pressure said and hugged her before walking her to the door and shutting it after she walked away.

Sulani Evans was living her best life.

THE SOUND of Sulani's phone ringing caught her attention. She grabbed it and saw that it was Gemini. "What's happinin', cuzzo?"

"Oh, nothingggg. I just called to check up on yo hoe ass." She giggled.

Sulani grinned. "Oh, whatever do you mean, dear cousin? I have no clue of what you're talking about." She said in a fake British accent.

"You so full of shit." Gemini laughed. "Not you in there lettin' the homies slut you out." She began cackling.

Sulani couldn't help but join in on her laughter. "Shit we all grown, right?"

"And are!" She agreed. "I know all that dick was hittin'!" Gemini said with a dreamy sigh.

Sulani bit her lip, reminiscing on the amount of pleasure she felt being fucked by two extremely attractive men. She had a ball. "Girl! I never would have thought! My holes still sore." She purred staring up dreamily at her living room ceiling. She was off work and relaxing.

"Sounds like you had a great time." She giggled. "Pressure comes home next week, I talked to him about and he was like he always wanted to fuck a C.O. so your timing in all of this was perfect. Good job Glen Coco!"

Sulani laughed and did an imaginary curtsey in her head. "Well, I'm glad I was able to contribute. Giiiirl, yo ass is in for a *killing* when that man touches down," she replied, remembering the way he had been fucking her ass the other night.

"And I can't fucking wait!" Gemini squealed. "I just wanted to fill you in on that though and to just say I love you, slut." She laughed lightly.

"I love you, too, crazy. Always." Sulani replied, and the two of them got off the phone.

Sulani was laying on the couch in nothing but a think tank top and some spandex shorts. Her mind began to drift. Thinking of everything that been happening to her over the last couple of months, so much had transpired, and she felt lost. Like she was only a shell of a former version of herself. She didn't know who she was anymore, and she didn't know what she wanted for herself.

The feelings that she was getting inside of her heart made her uncomfortable and anxious. She needed something to do. Picking up her phone, Sulani dialed a number.

"Wassup, Mrs. Officer," Zyan's deep baritone met her ears.

She couldn't help but crack a smile, "You busy?"

"Nah, wassup?"

She sighed. "I just wanted to say thank you for... because a comfort to me, lately."

"Oh... it ain't nothin', Su. You good wit' me, so I'ma be here." His voice was gentle when he spoke.

"I appreciate that..."

"You okay?" He asked.

She sighed again. "I don't know..."

"Talk to me..."

"I just been going through a lot. I'm not happy with where

I am with my life... I'm not sure I wanna be a C.O. anymore, but it's all that I know..."

Zyan was quiet. He was listening.

"I just don't know what I want to do moving forward. I don't know what I want for myself. For so long, I just did what I knew made my dad happy. And now that he's gone... I feel like I have no sense of purpose. And the reason I was with Dolo was because my dad liked him, but I couldn't stand his ass..."

"I can kind of relate to that..." Zyan added in softly.

"Yeah... and can I be honest?"

"Of course," he said as if it was obvious.

"Me moving the way that I have been with you is... reckless. I been going around fucking on you raw, you done came in me and all kinds of shit... I don't *do* that. I just been stressed out and got to doing just anything. Running away from my problems. Having meaningless sex to just distract myself from what's going on within' me internally. I realized that I feel numb inside." Her voice sounds sad by the end of her call. "And I feel bad about what happened with the fight... You ain't deserve that. I knew that nigga was gonna find out about us and I was just being selfish and not thinking."

She took a long pause. Zyan kept quiet understanding that she was venting to him. Sometimes an ear was all that a person needed. It warmed his heart because he truly could relate as he had been thinking about the same shit earlier that day.

"I just wanted to apologize about that, that's all. I owe you that. You know... they have footage of the incident. I could get that to you, and you and Zyan can sue. Just let me know."

The last tidbit of information caught Zyan by surprise. He knew that there were cameras, but he figured that Dolo would have been smart enough to take him to an area where there weren't any. *Dumbass.*

"I would appreciate that, Su. Thanks." He paused for a bit. "And you're right. I been moving reckless, too. It's crazy you said that because I was thinking the same shit... I been trying to distract myself as well to keep me from thinking about the shit that I have going on with my girl. I lowkey been using you to... not hurt her... maybe that is what it is, I don't really know how I feel about it... but yeah... I haven't been caring enough. I know I gotta work on that."

"Right..." Sulani paused, feeling lighter. "I appreciate you. You're a good friend, Zyan."

He chuckled. "That you way of telling me we're just friends?"

"Yes." She giggled.

"Of course," he chuckled. "I feel you though, you're a good friend, too, Sulani. I appreciate you more. For real. I do gotta question though..."

"Hm?"

"We can still fuck, right?" She could hear the grin in his voice.

She laughed. "I was gonna ask you the same thing. Shit, if you wit' it then I am..."

"When you came back to work again?"

A WEEK LATER, Zyan was settling himself behind Sulani, pressing his hard dick against her ass and immediately slipping a hand into her pants and between her thighs. after she closed his cell door. Pressure had left earlier in the week and Sulani was able to pull some strings to have Zyan in a cell on his own.

He brought his lips to her ear as he pushed pants down with his free and pressed on her lower back, making her bend over and brace her hands against the door so he could rub her wet pussy from behind.

"I been thinkin' about this pussy all damn day..." His words made her rain down on his hand as he slowly worked two fingers in and out of her wetness.

Losing herself in his touch, she closed her eyes, loving the feeling of his long fingers stroking in and out of her tightness.

"Your fingers feel so fuckin' good to me, Zyan." He always knew exactly what to say to turn her to putty in his hands.

It was the moment when he pulled his fingers from her pussy and then slowly slid his dick deep inside of her soon after that confirmed his need to fill her was still just as a strong as hers.

With every slow stroke that he fed her weeping pussy, she moaned. "Zyan." She moaned his name, making him groan.

"Look at you, Su. You're fuckin' sexy." His words in her ear were enough to start a familiar swirling in the pit of her stomach.

Her eyes were squeezed shut as she felt everything that he was doing to her body. "Fuck me harder, baby." Her words came out airy and short.

Holding onto her hips, he gave her what she wanted. Thrusting harder and faster in and out of her, he groaned when he felt her pussy start spasming around his hard dick as she let go.

"God yes! Fuck you feel so good! I missed this dick so much." Sulani cried, still bent over taking the delicious beating that her man was delivering to his pussy.

"Damn, I missed this shit too. Pussy tight as fuck, and you take it so good." He praised her.

She whimpered when he pulled out of her and then yelped when he scooped her up into his arms and gently placed her on the bed and spread her thighs apart before diving headfirst between them.

She moaned beneath him, a smile lighting up her face because she loved the feeling of his mouth on her. She didn't know what she loved more, him fucking her with his dick, or him fucking her with his mouth.

They had only had sex a couple of times, but she could hands down say that he was the best that she ever had, and after their first time together, she felt like she had just become addicted.

"Good, cause I love eating this shit." His words were almost a growl before he put his mouth back on her.

He teased her entrance with the tip of his tongue. He grabbed her by the thighs to hold her in place when she started to squirm under him. It only encouraged him to eat her more vigorously.

A loud cry fell from her lips when he pulled back slightly and spit on her clit. The more they got to know each other and had more sex, the nastier he seemed to get.

He proved that when he watched his saliva drip down her lips and sliding down the crack of her ass. Looking up, his dick jumped when he locked eyes with her. His dark eyes twinkled as he slid his hands under her cheeks and lifted her ass of so that he could swipe his tongue across her asshole.

"Zyannn."

With a groan, he pulled away from her and quickly stood to his feet and lined his dick up at her wet entrance. Without hesitation, he forced his dick back into her tightness. He needed to be inside of her.

He had been able to quickly pick up on what she liked because it's what he liked. She was a big girl and had already proven that she could take all that he had to offer. There was no longer a need for him to act like he wouldn't respectfully disrespect the pussy.

Zyan Jackson was a nasty ass nigga and he had finally found his match. He was convinced.

Thrusting in and out of her, he gripped her by the hips and pulled her into him with every thrust. Their eyes were locked on one another, communicating silently.

Skin slapping together, moans, and groans filled the room as Zyan fucked the stress that had been building up in -both of them over the last couple of weeks.

With a groan, he leaned down and wrapped his arms around Sulani, and kissed her deeply, slipping his tongue in her mouth. A hand came up and fisted itself in her hair and she moaned loudly in response.

Sulani moaned something incoherently. She could hardly speak because it felt so good when he rolled his hips into her, stretching and filling her in the most delectable way.

"Fuck!" He groaned loudly, burying his face in the crook of her neck. "This pussy always gonna make me cum."

He didn't want it to be over yet, he would stay right there inside of her if she could. In her. *With her.* Is where he belonged. Or at least that's how he felt at that moment.

"Cum with me, Su." He grabbed her hands, intertwined their fingers, before putting them both above her head.

"Okaaaay." She drew out, thrusting her hips into his, meeting him thrust for thrust, stroke for stroke.

"God, Sulani you make a nigga weak."

She gasped as he thrusted so deep into her, she felt like she could feel him in her chest. She couldn't breathe, and she didn't care, the pleasure that he was bringing her was more important than getting oxygen into her lungs.

In just a matter of weeks, the man inside of her had planted more than just his dick and seeds inside of her.

He had planted true and genuine companionship inside of her. Something she never felt before and was quickly and easily swallowing her whole. And she was letting it consume her.

What the two of them had was easy, authentic, and not complicated. It was everything that they both needed at that time.

"I needed you..." His whispered words in her ear sent her over the edge. Her pussy spasmed and clenched even tighter around his dick. A muffled scream left her, at the same time Zyan groaned and stilled as he released hard into her, fulling her with his seed.

She didn't know it, but he had just planted something inside of her that would bind them together forever, and beyond human comprehension.

Letting go of her hands, he collapsed on top of her and held her in his arms. He kissed her tenderly, his heart swelling and his eyes closed until he his heart rate had returned to normal. Opening up his eyes, he smiled lazily when he looked down at Sulani and saw her shaking her head back and forth in disbelief.

He pulled her closer and kissed the top of her head before getting settled on his back, with one arm wrapped underneath her, and the other hand behind his head. He stared blankly at the ceiling, his thoughts racing.

He didn't know where the state of his relationships were heading... but he was happy to have gained a new friend.

He was ready to experience something new and different. He looked at Sulani who was staring up at the top bunk.

I think I may have found it...

THE END

Did you enjoy the read?
Let us know how much by leaving us a review on Amazon and Goodreads.

Keep reading for a preview of...

Ridin' For You
By Telia Teanna

CHAPTER 1

"Shit, I gotta answer this." Zyair put his long-tattooed index finger to his lips, quietly shh-ing her.

McKenzie looked up at him with amused eyes and opened her mouth wider, taking more of his thick dick into her mouth. His lips parted and his hips slightly thrusted up into her mouth.

He was naked from the waist down. His onyx skin caused her mouth to water with the way that the sun shined through the large floor to ceiling windows of the condo he bought her recently.

"Wassup, baby?"

From her knees McKenzie's eyes shined bright with mischief as she watched her fuck buddy try not to moan while he was on the phone with his fiancée. She could hear her on the other side ask him where he was, so she purposely gagged on his dick, making him inhale sharply.

"Oh shit," he mumbled under his breath, tangling a big hand in the expensive Peruvian bundles that he had bought her also.

"Nothin'. I'm just taking a shit."

McKenzie choked on his dick because she laughed. This nigga ain't shit. She was laughing on the inside. Only a dumb bitch would believe some shit like that. Niggas don't take shit outside their houses.

He bit his lip and nodded down at McKenzie, humor lighting up his normally empty eyes. He knew that she always got off on doing nasty shit to him while he was on the phone with his bitch.

He'd be a lying ass nigga if he said that he never planned some of the calls between them. Her pussy was soaking wet every time. Even at that moment he knew she was enjoying every moment of him being on the phone while she sucked him off. She was playing with that little wet pussy, and it only made him grow harder in her mouth.

"How was your day, babe?" He asked. He knew that if he asked, she was going to talk his ear off for the next twenty minutes before asking if he was paying attention.

"Weeeell, I went to the mall today, right?" He muted his mic and dropped it on the couch.

"I'm funny to you, huh?" McKenzie's bronze eyes met his

almost black ones and winked at him, taking his long dick down her throat, swallowing him.

"Fuuuuuck," he moaned, sinking further into the couch and spreading his legs wider apart.

That trick right there was the very reason why he could never leave her ass alone. He couldn't imagine a life where he couldn't get his whole dick swallowed the way she did it. No other bitch had been able to do so, and he doubted that another bitch could.

"Mmmm," she moaned around his shaft when he tangled both his hands in her hair and thrusted in and out of her throat, moaning loudly.

That was another thing that was special about McKenzie, she was with whatever pleased him sexually. She basically let him use her as his personal fuck doll.

Yes, he had a whole girl at home that he was going to be marrying in just a few months, but there was no fucking way that he could exist in life without McKenzie's sex. She was the only one that could ever completely satiate him. And truthfully, he didn't care that he had a woman that worshipped the ground that he walked on at home.

The two could have made the perfect couple, but McKenzie didn't want to be tied down.

He groaned. "Fuck, I love this throat." He licked his lips and removed his hands from her head to let her breath.

The way his wet dick slid out of her throat, and she looked

up at him with "fuck me" eyes and for a second, he lost his train of thought and saw nothing but her.

"Better answer her." Her sultry voice broke him from his trance.

McKenzie chuckled and slapped his big black dick against her tongue. She loved the attention and intensity that he gave her when she was making him feel good. She didn't know why but she loved sucking Zyair's dick so much, that sometimes she'd meet up with him when he was out in the field just so that she could get a taste of him and hear him moan her name.

She was his fucking weakness, and she knew it. It was one of the many perks of having a baller ass nigga like Zy. His fire ass pipe game was another perk. Her favorite perk.

He picked up the phone and unmuted it. "What you say, babe?"

"I asked what kind of flowers did you think that we should get for the wedding?"

Her question immediately irritated him. He didn't fucking know, nor did he care. He was busy trying to buss a nut down his side bitch's throat.

"You know I don't knooooow-" he drew out the words at the exact moment McKenzie released his dick from her mouth, lifted his balls and one of his legs, and licked his gooch.

"What the heck are you doing?"

He couldn't mask the moans that left him as she teased the sensitive space between his anus and balls.

McKenzie laughed against his flesh when she heard his girl going off.

"You're with that bitch, aren't you?" She was livid.

McKenzie pulled away from him and laughed out loud. "He is, hoe. Now get the fuck off the phone so I can finish eating our nigga's ass, bitch," she taunted her.

"Zyair! You just gonna-" He hung up the phone.

"You always gotta fuckin' start some shit, Kenzie. Why you ain't just be quiet?" He huffed annoyed. He didn't feel like arguing with his bitch when he got home.

"'Cause I ain't feel like it." She winked at him and lowered herself onto her hands and knees. "Now, scoot down."

She didn't dare reach out to pull him further off the couch so she could reach her designation easier, he always threw a fit when she did. He'd go off on a rant talking about him being a grown ass man and not to handle him like he was some kind of bitch.

"I'ma stop fuckin' with you one day, I swear." He adjusted himself on the couch and pulled his shirt off and lifted one foot onto the couch, giving her better access to his ass.

"Is you?" She teasingly flicked her tongue across his asshole, and watched it pucker in response.

"Hell nah." He groaned and grabbed her by the back of the head and pressed her face back into his ass.

His eyes rolled into the back of his head. The fact that she ate his ass was another reason he'd never leave her alone.

Before Zyair met McKenzie, he never let a bitch anywhere

near his ass. He wasn't with that gay shit, but he soon learned that when it came to McKenzie, she had no boundaries. If she wanted to do something, she was going to do it, and whoever she was dealing with was going to like it. And after the first time she licked that spot and gave him a rim job, he was hooked.

Eating his ass is what got her the big ass condo with a stunning view, she was eating his ass in.

"Mmm, jack my dick, babe."

She did as he instructed and wrapped both of her hands around his length and stroked him while repeatedly swirling her tongue around his asshole. His sexy moans and groans made her pussy drip for him. She couldn't wait to feel him inside of her. One thing she absolutely loved was seeing Zyair's controlling ass, losing his shit as she sucked and fucked him the way only some type of sex demon could.

"Oh shit, I'm gonna blow." His hands reached around to cup around hers and jerk him faster.

McKenzie removed her tongue from his ass and wrapped her mouth around the head of his dick, anxiously waiting to taste him.

He groaned loudly and shot his load into her warm mouth. His toes curled, heart raced, and dick throbbed. She made him cum harder than any other bitch that he had ever fucked. His ass wasn't going anywhere.

After swallowing his load, she sexually licked her lips, smiling at the visual of Zyair in all of his black ass glory. Just scrumptious. He flashed her a boyish grin that reminded her of his youthful age. He was heavy in the streets, so it made him a lot older than what he was. That's what pressure from the streets did to a young nigga.

She fought the urge to grin back, and instead straddled his lap. His phone rang and they both looked at it to see his girl calling again. He flipped the phone so she couldn't see the screen and muted it.

"Don't worry about the phone. Come put that pussy in my face." He slapped her ass and watched her every movement while she climbed onto his face, mounting his tongue with a long moan.

Zyair wasted no time, stroking her large clit with gentle flicks. McKenzie had a bigger clit than any woman that he had ever been with. He used to think that it was a little weird. It was like licking on a small gumball, but he eventually embraced it and grew to love it.

Because her clit was so big, she was a lot more sensitive than any other woman he'd been with. Whenever he was licking on it, it made her go crazy on the dick after. It also helped that he genuinely enjoyed tasting her, especially since he didn't eat women out. Not even his fiancée. McKenzie though? That was some cake he'd never turn down. He devoured it every time.

His phone rang again, and a sneaky grin spread across her face. She leaned forward to grab his phone and answered it, putting it on speaker.

"Will you stop callin'?"

"You're one bold bitch. You just love being slutted out by my man, don't you?"

McKenzie laughed, and then moaned loudly when he pinched her clit between his thick, dark lips. "'The fuckin' boldest. I ain't the one being slutted out, baby. Why the fuck you think this nigga can't stay away from me?"

Zyair moaned against her flesh, his dick hardening at her talking her shit. She was that bitch and couldn't nobody tell her shit. He loved it.

"Just because you're willing to let him treat you like some whore on the street doesn't mean anything, baby girl. At the end of the day, I'm the one that he put a ring on. This little thing y'all have going on won't last long. As soon as we're married, you'll be history, babe."

McKenzie laughed. She's delusional.

She hissed and ground her fat clit roughly against his wet tongue. She purposely moaned into the phone's mic.

"Girl, bye! You got that ring, because I didn't want it, bitch. Stop fucking playing with me. He's only your man because I let you have him, hoe!"

The more shit she talked, the harder he got, and the faster he ate her pussy. There was something so fucking sexy about his women fighting over him. He knew who his dick was rooting for, though.

"Yeah, you keep telling yourself that, sweetie. Will you put my man on the phone now?"

McKenzie moaned before responding. "Can't. He's eating and has his mouth full."

Zyair met her bronze eyes. She saw nothing but pure and unadulterated lust staring back at her. She grinned down at him.

He got off on her talking shit to his girl just as much as she did. She always knew just what he liked and how to help him take his orgasms to the next level.

"I'm gonna whoop your ass when I see you."

"I'm waiting hoe. You know where I be at." And with that, McKenzie hung up the phone and brushed one of her hands down the fade of his head.

Zyair gave her clit a few firm strokes with the tip of his tongue, and she imploded on his face.

"Why you so mean to my girl, Ken?" He asked when he unattached his lips from her pussy and licked and sucked the inside of her thighs.

"Why you let me be mean to your girl, Zy?" It was a legitimate question.

"Don't try to turn your fucked up-ness around on me."

"Ain't nobody doing shit. Every time you come around here wanting me to fuck and suck on you, your bitch wants to come starting shit with me. So, you damn right I'm mean to that bitch. The fuck you think I am, Zy?"

Her toffee skin flushed red, a sign that she was getting upset. He got up from his seated position and pushed her onto her back and settled himself between her legs, lining his thick dick up at her entrance.

"You right. Imma check her when I get home." He rubbed the head of his dick teasingly back and forth across that juicy clit of hers.

"You better. I'd hate to have to cut you off." She threatened through a moan, her pussy leaking in anticipation for him to fill her.

"You gone cut me off?" He slowly sank into her. She was so tight, wet, and warm that he had to throw his head back and really enjoy the feel of what he was convinced to be the best pussy in the world. That tight muthafucka made him feel like he was the luckiest nigga in the world to be blessed with such a wonderful experience.

"I will if I have to." She moaned and used her thumb to thrum her clit.

He pushed her hand away and replaced it with his own and caught on to a rhythm and slowly long stroked her. He wanted her to feel every inch of his big dick and remember why she couldn't stop fucking him just as much as he wouldn't stop fucking her.

"Yeah? You don't want me to put this dick in your stomach no more?"

She said nothing, so he pulled completely out of her and then slammed back into her roughly. "Huh?"

"No," she said through a moan.

Zyair rolled his eyes and slapped her inner thigh. "You fulla shit, but okay."

He pulled out of her and stood to his feet. Smirking down at her and picking her up, he threw her over his shoulder and walked out to the balcony. The sun was starting to set, and the heat of the day was finally starting to cool down.

McKenzie giggled as she slumped over his shoulder. She didn't know why, but his ass loved tossing her around and she let him.

They were both butt ass naked as he rested her on her feet to look out at the amazing view of the city, at that time. She had neighbors that only needed to look out of their windows to see them, but they didn't give a fuck. They've fucked for audiences before.

Kenzie took a deep breath amazed at the view every time she was out there. She was grateful for it. Her hands gripped the iron railing, and her lips parted when she felt the heat of his body envelope her. One of his hands grabbed her hip, making her arch her back, and his other hand gripped his dick, as he fed it into her pussy.

Her body melted into him as soon as he entered her. He rested his face into the crook of her neck, holding her closely. The sounds of his moans in her ear making her wetter with every long, slow stroke.

"You like the view, baby?" He was curious.

He had been doing some house shopping with Kristina

when he saw it. His fiancée didn't want any kids, so she wanted to move into a condo.

When they viewed it together, Kristina had fallen head over heels for the property. It was lavish, in a great area with a great view. Truly fit for a queen. Too bad she wasn't the queen he felt was worthy enough of it.

As soon as he stepped inside and saw the large open concept, updated appliances, and the balcony, he knew that he was going to cop it for McKenzie. He knew that she was going to love it, and she did. She sucked his dick and ate his ass extra nastily the night he picked her up and surprised her with it.

"I love it, Zyair. Thank you." She turned her head so that she could kiss him.

He thrusted into her harder, making her moan every time he hit bottom.

"The world is yours, baby." And she believed him.

She knew that if she asked him for anything, he wouldn't hesitate to give it to her. If she called, he came running. When it came down to it, Zyair was the most consistent and reliable person in her life.

"A nigga just wishes that he was able to wake up in this bitch with you every morning and slide in this pussy." His hand drifted between her legs, thrumming her clit again.

McKenzie clutched the railing tighter and moaned. "You 'bout to marry a whole different woman, Zy."

He pumped into her harder, applying pressure to both her g-spot and her mental. "Whose fault is that?"

"Not mine!" She tried to pull away from him, but instead he pushed her into the railing and forcefully bent her over it. Her eyes widened and her heart raced in her chest as she looked at the large, jagged edges of rocks fifteen feet below.

Zyair grabbed the railing, trapping her so that he could pound hard and fast into her. "Say the word, Kenz. Say it and I swear to God, I'll throw that bitch out like a dirty dish rag."

Her eyes rolled into the back of her head. He was hitting just the right spot that had her squirting all over his dick with each stroke. She didn't answer him just focused on how good he was making her feel.

"Look at this pussy wetting me up. You don't wanna wake up and go to sleep like this, Kenz? You don't want this?" He grabbed her around the throat and pulled her up so that her back was touching his chest.

She looked out at the view, and watched the sun set and all the city lights turn on in the distance as it began to darken. It was literally the most beautiful, erotic, and dare she say romantic thing she had experienced in her life. Tears welled in her eyes as she felt an orgasm swirling around in her gut, making her body tremble hard against him.

He had managed to get into her head, and she was fighting hard to not go there with him. She hated when he brought up them becoming more than what they were. She couldn't understand why he just couldn't keep things as they were.

"You don't want us, McKenzie?" His voice broke in the middle of his sentence.

"I'm cumming." Her words came out in a rush and through a moan as she let go.

Her orgasm prompted his and he released deep inside of her with a loud groan. The two took a few moments to catch their breaths.

"Why you don't wanna be with me, McKenzie? Why am I never good enough for you?" He pulled out of her and took a few steps back.

McKenzie remained in the same position against the balcony railing. She stared blankly out at the view in front of her, tears freely streaming down her face. She remained quiet. After a minute or two of silence, Zyair shook his head and turned to go back inside and put his clothes on. He knew that she wasn't going to answer him. She never did when he brought it up. And every time he did, his heart broke a little bit more each time.

He took his time showering and dressing. He was putting his Rolex back on his wrist when he emerged from her bedroom. McKenzie was on the couch nursing a drink, the sounds of H.E.R. playing softly from the speakers built into the ceiling throughout the place. She was in a satin robe with her toffee legs tucked beneath her. He wanted nothing more than to just stay and be with her. They didn't even have to fuck all night like they normally did. He just wanted to be held by her, while they went back and forth roasting each other.

But he needed to go. His feelings were hurt, and he didn't want her to know it. Shit, he brought it on himself. He knew that she wouldn't give him a real answer as to why she didn't want to be exclusively his. It never stopped him from asking in hopes that he had somehow proved that he was worthy of her heart.

He made his way over to the couch where he had left his phone. The two of them locked eyes when he neared her. She held his phone out for him to take.

"You're more than enough, Zyair. Always have been." Her voice was horse from crying.

"Then what's the problem?" He was genuinely confused.

She diverted her eyes, and he took a seat next to her on the couch and clasped his hands together.

"I'm the one who isn't good enough, Zy. Kristina though? She's good for you. Nice, gorgeous, intelligent, all of that. I don't have shit to offer you but ass."

In the two years he and McKenzie had been fucking around, he'd never heard her so sad and serious. He hated that she felt that way and was comparing herself to his girl when there was no need. It also didn't sit well with him that she kept downplaying herself. He had never known her to be the insecure type, but that's exactly how she sounded in that moment, and he felt guilty for it.

"That's not true," he protested.

She rolled her eyes and took a sip of her henny and coke.

"It is, but okay. We don't even know each other like that and you talking about moving in here together."

His head jerked back. "Woah, we been fuckin' for two years, Kenz. How the hell do we not know each other? We ain't strangers, nigga."

"Exactly! We been fuckin'. That's it! We know nothing about each other outside of how we like to have sex."

His face was screwed up as he tried to process what she was saying. "That's bullshit."

She sighed and ran her fingers through her bundles. "What's my last name, Zyair?"

Silence.

She took another sip of her drink. "When's my birthday?"

"We celebrated your birthday together this year."

"Okay?" She raised an eyebrow at him and shifted so that she could look at him directly. "You should know when it is then, right?"

Damn. He had to think back and make a guess. "Uh, it's in March, right?" He scratched his head.

"No. You get my point, yet?"

He sighed and ran a hand down his face. "No. I never remember shit like that. That typa shit ain't important."

"That's why more will never be able to become of us, Zyair. That kind of shit is important to me. I don't wanna commit to you and then be disappointed that it's not all sugar and rainbows. There's a whole lot of shit that comes with fuckin' with a nigga like you. Being deemed yours in a city that you run will force me to be trapped in a bubble for many different reasons, none of which I'd care to experience."

"You know you've always been safe with me, McKenzie." That was a concern that he heard from women that he was involved with. It was a concern that Kristina constantly brought up to him when she tried to convince him to get out of the dope game and go legit.

His career of choice was in a dangerous industry. Niggas wanted his head everywhere he went and were willing to hurt anyone attached to him. The women he was with always wanted the benefits, but then got scared and ran when the risks got too risky. He thought that McKenzie was different and that she would be able to handle what came with his lifestyle. He was quickly becoming disappointed to know that everything that he had perceived her to be was the exact opposite.

"I'm not worried about street shit. I tote pistols too, nigga. I ain't never feared death. Six months ago, you proposed to me, and I said no. I didn't think you were ready for marriage. I still don't think you're ready. I don't even think that you are the marriage type at all. And you proved it to me when two months after turning you down, I look on fucking Instagram and see some preppy bitch with the ring you tried to give me on her finger, posted on your page."

She paused to calm herself down. Her voice was strained as she spoke, her emotions getting the best of her. He sat quietly, mentally kicking his own ass for the dumb shit that he had done.

"You like drama, Zyair. Cool, if that's what you want to do, fine. I get off on arguing and showing my ass in front of your bitches sometimes, too. It's been fun. But I'm damn near thirty, this shit is getting old. My feelings are involved, and honestly, you giving that bitch my ring, hurt like hell. Being with you will mean that everybody knows that I'm yours. Therefore, making me off limits, cause the niggas in this city is mad pussy and never go against you. And at the same time, you can still, and more than likely will still be out in the streets doing you. I'm not that dumb of a bitch, Zyair. If we go there, I know for a fact that I will lose you the same damn way I got you. That's how karma works."

She finished off the rest of her drink.

He sighed and sat back against the couch, thinking. She had a few points. He wanted to tell her that she had everything wrong but figured that he should just keep it to himself until they were more emotionally under control.

"I'm just gonna go." He had a whole lot that he wanted to say, but the timing was off.

They needed some time apart, so he was going to give her that. She was nodding her head when he stood up. Her eyes were staring blankly out of the living room window, and she stayed in that position until she heard the front door close, and finally, she let the tears fall down her face.

Available Now On All Platforms

OTHER BOOKS BY

<u>URBAN AINT DEAD</u>

Tales 4rm Da Dale

The Hottest Summer Ever

Hittin' Licks For The Holidays: Atlanta

Wet Dreams On Lockdown: The Nurse

By **Elijah R. Freeman**

Despite The Odds

By **Juhnell Morgan**

Good Girl Gone Rogue

By **Manny Black**

Hittaz

Hittaz 2

Hittaz 3

Hittaz 4

Coldhearted

By **Lou Garden Price, Sr.**

Charge It To The Game

Charge It To The Game 2

A Summer To Remember With My Hitta

Snatched Up By A Hitta

Santa Sent Me A Real One For Christmas

Wet Dreams on Lockdown: The Unit Manager

By **Nai**

A Setup For Revenge

Wet Dreams On Lockdown: Librarian

By **Ashley Williams**

Ridin' For You

Trickin' on a Heaux for Christmas: A BBW Love Story

Homie Hoppin' For The Holidays

By **Telia Teanna**

The State's Witness

The State's Witness 2

The State's Witness 3

By **Kyiris Ashley**

Stuck In The Trenches

Stuck In The Trenches 2

By **Huff Tha Great**

The Swipe

By **Toōla**

Melted the Heart of a Menace

By P. Wise

Merry Trapmas: Ice & Frost

By **Mia Sky**

Thug Me The Right Way

By **DiamondATL & Nai**

Wet Dreams on Lockdown: The Male C.O

By **Tamyra Griffin**

Wet Dreams On Lockdown: The Counselor

By **Paris Iman**

Wet Dreams On Lockdown: The Warden

By **Shawnice**

Wet Dreams On Lockdown: The Captain

By **TN Jones**

BOOKS BY

URBAN AINT DEAD's C.E.O

<u>Elijah R. Freeman</u>

Triggadale

Triggadale 2

Triggadale 3

Tales 4rm Da Dale

The Hottest Summer Ever

Murda Was The Case

Murda Was The Case 2

Murda Was The Case 3

Hittin' Licks For The Holidays: Atlanta

Wet Dreams On Lockdown: The Nurse

STAY CONNECTED

Follow

Elijah R. Freeman

On Social Media

FB: Elijah R. Freeman

IG: @the_future_of_urban_fiction

www.ingramcontent.com/pod-product-compliance
Lightning Source LLC
Chambersburg PA
CBHW071159300726
48975CB00004B/1217